M000223202

My Forever Cocky Biker Encounter

Concrete Angels MC Book 1

Siobhan Muir

Copyright © 2019 Siobhan Muir

All rights reserved.

ISBN: 1-947221-11-6
ISBN-13: 978-1-947221-11-6

DEDICATION

Dedicated to all the authors and readers who tirelessly fought the attempted trademark on the words Cocky, Forever, Biker, Encounter, and Rebellion. No one should steal words from general use just to get a little attention.

ACKNOWLEDGMENTS

Writing a book is never really a one-person job, and writing a series is especially difficult alone. Keeping track of details is so much easier when you have help. Not only does it take a great deal of hard work, editing, and research on the part of the author to get things correct, but without my compatriots, there'd be a lot more mistakes. Any mistakes are my own.

Great thanks to Paige Prince for editing and making sure I knew what these handguns looks like and how they work. Thanks to Simon Cooki who embodied the face of Scott Free. You were totally perfect for this character! And great thanks to Kris Norris for designing the cover with such a tough image to balance. You rock.

As always, great thanks to my readers for cheering me on. Y'all make my writing worth the detailed effort.

CHAPTER ONE

Oriana

"We're gonna stage a rebellion."

"A what?" I looked over at Melinda and wondered what she was going on about.

"A rebellion. It's gonna be epic."

I shook my head. Don't get me wrong. I'd been known to be rebellious. I went out without a bra on because I'd read about these studies that showed boobs were perkier if you left the bra off, and my boobs needed some perky. I didn't like Miracle Whip, Cool Whip, or Whipped Cream in a can. I refused to keep the tags on my mattresses and pillows, and I only changed my car's oil every five thousand miles rather than every three thousand. But an epic rebellion?

"Against what?"

"Cocky bikers."

I rolled my eyes. "Sweet glory. Are you back with Roy again?" Her on-again-off-again relationship with her boyfriend made Jerry Springer's show look positively tame.

"No, I'm done with him and the Concrete Angels MC,

which is why we're gonna stage the rebellion."

I sighed and rubbed my forehead. She'd said something to that effect before. I didn't take her seriously. I couldn't. Melinda was the type of woman where everything that went wrong turned her into a spitting drama llama. I could barely keep up on the best days. But when she dove into full-on diva screamer, I usually ducked and covered.

I shouldn't ask. Just let it go, Oriana. "What did he do this time?"

Melinda snarled, her eyes going wide and her nostrils flaring. "What did he do? He decided to go to his club's rally in Cheyenne during our anniversary."

At this point, she'd broken up with him so many times, I couldn't keep track of their anniversary, and I doubted Roy could either.

"What the fuck is in Wyoming, anyway? It's like prairie dogs and sage brush." She shook her head, her lips pulled back from her teeth. "Oh, no. It's not what he did. It's what he *didn't* do. He *didn't* ask me if I wanted to come along. He *didn't* ask me if it was okay to go without me. He *didn't* ask me—"

"How to wipe his ass and tie his shoes?" I raised an eyebrow. "Gee, I can't imagine why that is."

She scowled at me. "Whose side are you on? You're supposed to be my friend."

"I *am* your friend, which is why I'm giving you tough love and telling you to cool down. He's a cocky biker, something you knew going into this…" I waved my hand in distraction. "Thing you have with him. And you've broken up with him more times than I can count, which is impressive because I'm a forensic accountant. Do you even remember the first time you started going out with him?"

"Of course, I do! It was…" She screwed up her face and I swore smoke rose from her ears. "That's not the point. The point is he should've asked me to go with him."

I took a deep breath and counted to ten before I gave

her a patient smile. "Maybe he thought you wouldn't want to go with him. Have you ever gone before?"

"No." Melinda shook her head. "But he never asked."

"How about you text him and ask if you could go with him? Or better yet, call him."

She gaped at me in horror. "I couldn't do that."

"Why not?"

"Because that would be butting into his business and I couldn't do that."

I snorted and dropped my chin. "But you're mad at him because he won't do what you want? Honey, you gotta pick your poison here. Just call him and ask if you can go with him."

"I can't. He turns off his phone when he gets ready to go on these trips." Melinda shook her hands in distress.

"So go to his clubhouse and talk to him. Or call one of his friends. Come on, don't go all damsel on me."

"Oh my gawd, I can't go over there by myself. I'm not wearing his patch. They'd eat me alive." She blanched white.

I remembered that the women in the motorcycle clubs often wore a vest with a patch or emblem on them showing to whom they belonged. In some ways it infuriated me. We were people, not belongings. But women everywhere did what they could to survive, and in MC clubs it was safer to be owned. I hated to think of what would happen to Melinda if she showed up without Roy's patch.

"You could come with me."

"What?" I damn near dropped my coffee mug, a crime punishable by death in my world. "Are you insane? I don't know any of them, not even Roy. I don't put myself in position of being around too many male strangers."

"Who's being the damsel now?"

"I'm being a pragmatist. They don't know me and I don't know them. To them I'd look like an offering with a pair of tits." I shook my head. "If I walk in there, I'm fair game, and I'm nobody's "old lady." That goes against everything I am."

"Come on, Oriana. It's not like it's a cult and if you walk in, you won't walk out." She wrinkled her nose. "You're only going to be there a few minutes while I talk to Roy, and then we'll be out of there."

"Not necessarily. You might go with him. Then how will I get out of there?" I shook my head, the coffee sitting in my gut like toxic waste. "No, that's nuts. It's got Hotel California written all over it. I'm not putting myself in the position of danger or incarceration. Call his friends."

"Pweeeze?" She batted her eyes at me and pouted, and I seriously wondered why the hell she was my friend. "Can't you just help me this one time? I gotta talk to him and this is the only way."

"Wait a minute. You said you were done with Roy and the Concrete Angels." I rose and headed for the sink. If I was going to put up with this crap, I seriously needed another cup of coffee and a hair tie. No one should have hair in their face when dealing with this level of manipulation.

"You were the one to change my mind."

"If you can change your mind, you can go by yourself. I'm sure he'd be delighted to see you." Personally, I had my doubts, but I wasn't about to put myself in the same position.

"It'll only be this once and I'll never ask you for anything again." Melinda batted her eyes and tried to look cute, but I stood my ground and she scowled. "Come on, you owe me. Remember when I took on those bullies at the grocery store, and helped get them fired for harassing you?"

My shoulders dropped with my brows. "Yes."

"And remember when I drove you all the way down to Pueblo, Colorado, just to make sure you got to see that car race?"

I scowled. "Yes." She'd done more than that. She'd financed the whole trip.

"I'm calling in my marker now. Please do this with me and I won't ask for anything ever again." She gave me a sweet, vacant smile and I gritted my teeth.

I doubted she wouldn't ask me for anything again, but I definitely owed her.

"All right. Fine. I'll go with you to the Concrete Angels' place, but I have to be back at work on Monday. I can't stay with them forever." I pointed my finger at her and narrowed my eyes. "Promise me you'll get me out of their compound before you ride into the sunset with Roy the roadie."

"Cross my heart and hope to die." Melinda gave me brilliant smile. "But I would pack a bag just in case."

That didn't bode well.

****

Oriana

The drive from Fort Collins to Skin Gulch, Colorado took roughly forty-five minutes. We drove westward into the Rocky Mountains and basically turned left at the fork onto Stove Prairie Road. The compound of the Concrete Angels sat a few hundred feet off the main road with a sliding steel gate and an actual guard shack beside it. The hard-eyed men who watched us arrive in Melinda's sporty little Kia had beards to make ZZ Top jealous. I swallowed hard and hoped they looked meaner than they actually were.

"Hey, Egyptian, can you let us in? I need to talk to Roy." She tipped her chin and smiled coyly.

The dark-haired man with a beaked nose and fathomless eyes stared past Melinda to me. I tried to keep my expression impassive, fear and unease locking my voice in my throat. *Sweet glory, I'm in so much trouble.*

He narrowed his eyes and lifted his chin at me. "Who's this?"

"This is my best friend Oriana. She's good with numbers."

Wait, what? My eyes widened as I transferred my gaze to the back of Melinda's head. *What does she mean I'm good with numbers?* Was this a setup? My gut sank. Shit-oh-dear, had my "best friend" broken up with her boyfriend as a ruse to get me to come up to the Concrete Angels' compound? Anger, betrayal, and fear did the do-si-do in my stomach.

"Huh." Egyptian looked me over like a tasty steak and a small smile curled his lips. "Okay. Go inside." He waved his hand and the steel gate slid open revealing a surprisingly elegant compound.

I expected old, crumbling double-wide, warehouse-like buildings. Instead, what I found was a well-maintained motel sort of setting. Several small cabins surrounded a central club house and a large aluminum barn. All of the buildings had clean lines and clean windows. A few even had stained glass artwork in their front windows. All the cabins sported flower window boxes with petunias and marigolds of various colors, and all the buildings were neatly painted.

This doesn't look like a biker gang hangout.

Melinda pulled up in front of the clubhouse and shot me a look bereft of smile.

"Now listen up. I brought you here because you're a wiz with numbers and the Concrete Angels have some money troubles. I told them I have a friend who could help."

"Thanks for the heads-up. When were you gonna ask me if I wanted to help?"

She raised her chin, not at all repentant. "They need your skills and I gave them my word. No one ever goes back on their word and lives to tell about it."

"Fan-fucking-tastic, Mel. But it wasn't your word to give." I scowled. "You didn't ask, you kidnapped me and made me think I was helping you. You lied and manipulated me into coming up here. What if I say no?"

She shot me a flat look. "You can't say no to the Concrete Angels."

"Oh, yes I can. You didn't ask if I wanted to help them, you just took me here. And I said I didn't want to come." I matched her stare for stare. "I also said they wouldn't let me leave. But you did it anyway. This is your mess, so get me out of it." I crossed my arms over my chest.

Melinda scowled, but she looked away and swallowed hard. "Oriana, you have to listen to me. They need your abilities and they don't take no for an answer." She met my gaze and I read real fear in her eyes. "I didn't have a choice in asking you to do this. I had to ask and I had to bring you. If I didn't, there would've been consequences I couldn't pay."

I shook my head. "Why are you involved with these people, Mel? Why would you stay with anyone who threatened your life like that?"

She tilted her head with a sad half-smile. "They kinda, sorta saved me at the lowest point in my life. I owe them."

I nodded slowly. "And now they own you."

She shrugged. "Come on, Oriana. It won't be that bad. Just one job and you'll be done."

I snorted. "You don't really believe that, do you?"

She laughed, but it didn't reach her eyes. "Nope."

"Right."

I bit my bottom lip and stared down at my lap. I'd gone all out today with a V-necked T-shirt with "$E=MC^2$ Enthusiasm = More Coffee Squared" emblazoned across my boobs, and denim capris. At least I'd worn my glasses and close-toed shoes. Too bad I hadn't brought my Sig

Sauer. Guess I'd grown a little lax since I'd left the FBI.

"Am I dressed okay before I meet the other cult members?"

Melinda scowled. "It's really not like that."

I raised an eyebrow and she grimaced.

"It doesn't matter. I packed you a bag."

"What the fuck, Mel?" I stared at her in horror. "Give me the keys." I held out my hand.

"What?" Her eyes widened.

"Give me the fuckin' keys. I'm getting myself out of this."

"No, you can't." She held them out of reach. "You have to do this and stay. That's why I brought the clothes."

"Mel, I'm not going to be held here against my will. Give. Me. The. Keys."

Her eyes filled with tears, but I wouldn't be swayed by her puppy-dog looks anymore. Who knew this woman was so manipulative? *I need to start thinking like an FBI agent again.*

"Please, Oriana."

"The keys. Now." I wouldn't let her guilt me. The situation had grown too dangerous.

Before she could do anything, someone knocked on the driver's side window. We both jumped, my heart galloping like an entire herd of bison. Panic flashed across Mel's face before she pressed the button to lower the window.

"Everything okay in there, Melrose?"

Melrose? What kind of a name is that?

The man on the other side of the door was tall, dark blond, and had the biggest nose I'd seen in a long time. He also had piercing blue eyes that seemed to see into my soul when he switched his gaze to me.

"Yeah, yeah, it's all good, Michael. We're just getting out." She shot me a meaningful look and opened her door.

"Melinda, no." I reached for her, but she slipped out of the car and I was stuck.

Aw hell, now what do I do? I couldn't stay in the car, but I didn't have the keys to make a run for it. Sure, I could hot-wire it. I'd learned that long before I joined the FBI. But I didn't want anything to happen to Melinda if I rabbited.

Before I could make a decision, my door opened and I looked up into Michael's earnest eyes. "You coming?"

"I—Yeah, coming."

Arguing wouldn't do any good and sitting in the car wouldn't give me a chance to assess my escape routes. Right now, I was stuck here until I figured out the lay of the land, and just what kind of mess Melinda had gotten me into.

I got out of the car, but stepped away from the man trying to take my arm. "I don't need a physical escort. Keep your hands to yourself, big guy."

"Michael." He tilted his head and gave me a half-smile. "You don't want to be here, do you?"

"What was your first clue? I don't like liars, cheats, or scammers. So far, my 'friend' has been at least two of the three. So keep your hands off me. Got it?"

He held his hands up as amusement creased his lips. "Roger that, Ms..." He waited for my name.

"Hunter."

He raised an eyebrow. "Ms. Hunter. Let me be the first to welcome you to the Concrete Angels."

"Oh, I'm not staying." I lifted my chin as his eyebrows went up. "I just need the keys so I can drive myself home."

One of the other men laughed, a harsh, grating sound that sent fear skittering up my spine. "Once you drive in, there ain't no drivin' out."

My gaze lasered into Melinda as she turned to look at me. "I told you this had Hotel California written all over it."

She didn't laugh. Her mouth tightened and her eyes rolled up in her head as she toppled backwards with a surprised sigh. My jaw dropped and I took a few steps toward her, away from the car, as she swooned like a friggin' damsel in a dress. Exclamations erupted from the men around us and someone caught her, carrying her toward the clubhouse, and leaving me with Michael and a new man who'd approached from behind.

"Who do we have here, Schnoz?"

I spun to identify the gravelly-voiced speaker, but when my gaze landed on him, I forgot everything about trying to get away. *Sweet glory, where the hell did he come from?*

He had close cropped hair, a cleft chin with scruff on it, and broad shoulders encased in a faded black T-shirt. But the eyes took my breath away. A rare color of seafoam green, most often seen in cats' eyes, stared into me from under arching brows and half-closed lids. He appeared sleepy and relaxed, but I bet those eyes missed nothing.

"Ms. Hunter, meet Scott Free."

"Mr. Free."

"Not mister, just Scott. As in scot-free, sweetheart." He smirked at me and anger surged in my chest.

"Not sweetheart, Hunter. I'm not your sweetheart, doll, honey, little lady, or darling. You don't need a pet name for me because I'm not your pet. Copy?"

If anything, his smirk grew. "Yes, ma'am. Copy that."

Yeah, I doubted it.

I rounded the car and reached for the rear door. Michael made a sudden move, his gaze more fierce than I'd seen at first. *Holy shit, he's got the intensity of...of...* My imagination failed me, but I stood my ground despite the unease prickling my arms.

"I'm getting my bag. Y'all gonna be as jumpy as cats the whole time I'm here or is that your usual?" I hoped my voice remained steady as I opened the door and pulled out the bag Mel had packed for me.

Scott grinned. "Don't worry about Michael. He's

always kinda twitchy around new girls."

I sighed and raised my chin before I met Scott's amused gaze. "Not a girl. I'm probably older than you are. Could you at least try not to be sexist for my benefit?"

I didn't bother to wait for his answer as I threw the bag over my head to hang across my body. Hey, I'm old enough to know not to carry it on one shoulder. I'd need the chiropractor the next day and from what I could tell, I wouldn't be leaving the compound anytime soon.

At least she brought my computer. When the hell had she packed all this stuff for me? I thought I was pretty observant, but I hadn't noticed her getting anything from my place. *Which probably means she'd already packed the go-bag.*

What I did notice was half the men still in the yard out in front of the clubhouse watched me with either covetous lust, or wary uncertainty. Except Michael and Scott. Michael wore a benevolent smile that didn't match his badass appearance, and Scott watched me as if I represented a puzzle he had to solve. *Good luck with that, buddy.* I had no intention of getting to know any of these people better.

"So, shall we get this show on the road? I have the second season of Blindspot to watch when I get home." I ran my gaze over Scott. "Come to think of it, you look a lot like Assistant Director Kurt Weller of the FBI. You sure you're not undercover or something?"

Scott snorted. "No such luck, sweetheart. No one's comin' to save you from the authorities."

"Oh, I know, *sweetheart.* I'll be saving myself when the time comes."

Scott threw back his head and laughed as Michael waved me toward the clubhouse. Despite his lack of faith in my as yet unknown abilities, I liked his laugh. The sensual quality to it had my body reacting in inappropriate ways. *I'm not falling for a biker who has enough gravel in his voice to be used for traction on icy roads.* I straightened my spine and headed through the door of the clubhouse.

Again, I was taken aback at the elegance of the space. Instead of a reception desk and sitting room, the walls had been cleared out to give space for two pool tables, one with green felt, the other with purple, a foosball table, a sixty-five inch flat screen TV, a bar, and an actual mechanical bull. A sign hanging over it read, "No Bullshit."

A few doors ringed the room. Some I suspected were actual bedrooms, but the others must have been offices, meeting rooms, and an infirmary, judging from the scent wafting out of it. I caught sight of Melinda sitting on an exam table speaking with someone who watched her with concern.

Yeah, right. Don't be fooled, buddy. She's a manipulative little bitch.

I turned my gaze away and focused on the man seated on a bar stool, facing me and my escorts. My world shifted sideways and I wondered if someone had cloned half the male actors of Hollywood and threw them into this biker club.

The man sitting on the bar stool wore jeans, dark green T-shirt, and a leather vest with a gargoyle emblem representing the Concrete Angels emblazoned across his back. The patch said "PREZ." He had thick brows, shoulder length reddish-brown hair and a matching trimmed beard, and blue eyes dark enough to be navy. His lips seemed creased into a perpetual smirk that I'd seen on the actor who played the God of Thunder in movies. I half expected him to have a soft, seductive Aussie accent as I stopped in front of him with my arms loose and one hand on my bag.

"You must be Oriana Hunter, *ja?*" The musical voice full of amusement rolled over me with a stark Norwegian accent.

I opened my mouth to give him a snarky response, but

something about this guy gave me pause. He didn't have a heavyset body or even the height of some of the others, but the energy emanating from him made the hair on the back of my neck rise. There was a reason he led the Concrete Angels, and I didn't want to test out why.

"Yes." I thought it best to go simple.

He tilted his head. "*Det er bra.* Melrose came through after all." He narrowed his eyes and a smirk curled his lips. "But you don't wanna be here, *ja?*"

What was it with all the guys saying that? "No."

"You know who we are?"

While his question seemed innocuous enough, something told me he asked more than the simple arrangement of the words. *Do I know they're known for being both saviors and perpetrators? Oh yeah. Thank you, FBI experience.*

"Yes."

He nodded as Michael hovered at his left shoulder. Scott stood to my left and his gaze burned into my side with the heat of the magnifying glass in the sun. What was his issue? Did I have paint on my face? Or was it just my boobs encased in fitted cotton?

Probably the boobs.

The leader spread his hands and gave a wide smile. "Welcome to the Concrete Angels. My name is Loki and you're under my protection."

Loki? He looked like the actor who played the God of Thunder in the movies, and that's the name he picked?

"Seriously?"

He smirked and shrugged. "They say I look like a character and started calling me this. It stuck."

"Right."

"Do you speak more than one-word answers?"

I narrowed my eyes. "Why?"

He threw back his head and laughed with real amusement, and despite his intense power, I relaxed. If the man could laugh at my snark, I might be able to survive this encounter. I caught Scott grinning while Michael smirked.

"Do you know why you're here, Oriana Hunter?"

I shook my head. "No, but I overheard Mel say y'all have had money troubles and you need someone good with numbers."

"She speaks!" Scott crowed before dissolving into a laugh.

I shot him a glare before returning my attention to Loki. "That true?"

Loki shrugged. "Not money troubles. More like money trickery. Melrose says you're a forensic accountant and can find money in places no one wants it found."

I looked around the room, cataloguing where everyone stood. I met Scott's eyes briefly but I didn't like the intensity in them. "Yeah, that's my profession. What do you need a forensic accountant for?"

Loki spread his hands. "To find money, of course."

I waved at the expensive toys around the room. "Looks like you're doing fine."

Loki's affability disappeared as if someone had flipped a switch and I shivered.

"Someone stole money from us and it cannot stand. We need you to find it and who has chosen to endanger his life in this way."

The energy of the room became dangerously charged. I half-expected some jackass to light a match and the whole house to go up. But I'd been in tighter and scarier situations when I worked for the FBI, so I locked my unease down and met his furious gaze.

"So, you want to hire me to scour your financial accounts and pinpoint who is stealing from you and how they did it?"

"*Ja*, hire you. With a contract and everything." He crossed his arms over his chest as the others around him nodded.

"You're offering me a contract?" It sounded like he was ordering a hitman. *Not that he needs one with all these sociopaths around him.*

"I'm hiring you as a freelancer to help with specific money issues. We should definitely get the terms down in writing." Loki tilted his head. "A contract ensures everyone abides by the rules."

"Including you?"

He smirked. "Especially me."

I nodded slowly. "Fine. You got someone to write these down? Because I have a few terms of my own."

His eyebrows went up. "Do you? Very well." He turned and waved to a quiet guy I'd missed in my perusal of the room. "Neo, write down the terms of our contract with Ms. Hunter. I don't want any details missed."

Neo had the same quiet presence as the actor who'd starred in that time travel movie where the teenagers had to do a history project and kept snagging the real people from history. He had dark eyes, a scraggly beard, and shoulder-length hair. He didn't look like he smiled often, but his body language conveyed thoughtful affability.

"So, what are your terms, Ms. Hunter?"

I met Loki's gaze as Neo sat down with a tablet. "I'm here to conduct a forensic accounting analysis of your financial accounts and records to determine if and where someone is embezzling from you. Correct?"

"So far." Loki nodded.

"I don't belong to anyone. I'm my own person and I'll be treated as such. I'm an equal in standing to all members of the Concrete Angels Motorcycle Club, and any actions to violate that such as unwanted molestation, sexual assault, harassment, will result in the termination of this contract. I'll be allowed to leave the compound with all my belongings and given safe passage to a location of my choosing."

Some of the men growled and moaned as if my requirements were unfair. Scott was the loudest. *Sorry guys, you'll have to respect me enough to keep your dicks in your pants.*

Loki nodded again, something resembling approval in his gaze. "Go on."

"I'll be housed in my own room or cabin. I won't stay in a dorm or barracks. I work at all hours and need privacy. I'll use it as an office. I'll need internet privileges and access to any paper or electronic financial records."

Neo's hands flew over the tablet. I'd never seen anyone hunt-and-peck as fast as he did, and I had to wonder if he had some sort of odd computer connection like the movie character. *Computer connection.* I narrowed my eyes.

"I also want to make sure there are no listening or viewing devices to spy on me in my office. That would be considered a breach in the contract and I'd be gone."

Neo paused and looked up at me, surprised I'd figured out his little gadgetry secret. *Oh yeah, big boy, I know you're the resident computer nerd. Goddess knows what all you've seen on the security cameras.* He shot a look at Loki and the other man waved acceptance.

Loki gave me a half smile. "Anything else?"

"Yeah, you're going to pay me time-and-a-half my going rate at my job because I'm obviously going to be gone a while. I can't live on smiles and motorcycle fumes. Hell, I might not have a job by the time I'm done with this, so I gotta know I have options." I raised my chin. "And I want dental."

"Dental?" Scott barked.

"You know how much root canals are these days? I'd have to take a loan out from the Russian mob, and you know how well those work out." I returned my gaze to Loki. "And when I've done the job, I want to be free to leave without repercussions or reprisals."

"I agree you'll be free to leave if you cannot reveal the financial secrets of the Concrete Angels." Loki looked at Neo as he typed.

I nodded. "That's reasonable. But I want it clear that you and all the members of the Concrete Angels, both national and all local chapters, will leave me alone after this. You won't send your trained messenger lady to reel me back in."

Loki tilted his head again. "What if you don't want to leave?"

I snorted. "Good luck with that."

CHAPTER TWO

Scott

I held back the laugh rumbling in my chest. *Hold it together, jackass.* Oriana Hunter was a spitfire, though she wasn't little. She stood nearly my height, six-four, and had golden eyes that spat sparks. No bullshit, they were the same color of the best whiskey I'd ever had. She dressed casual in a denim capri pants and a tee that showed enough cleavage to make my cock swell and my balls tighten up. But she ruled that fuckin' room with her presence. Loki was badass, no question about it, but Oriana held her own. *Damn, I need to get me some of that.*

Except she'd made it clear in her contract no one could hook up with her. The one term with wiggle room was 'unwanted.' All I had to do was get her to want me and my affections, and we'd be home-free. *Aw yeah.* I just had to figure out how.

Loki glanced up at me and gave me a half-smile I'd learn to dread. *Aw hell, what's he thinking about now?* But our enigmatic leader only looked back at Oriana as she read over the terms Neo had typed up on his tablet.

"Looks good to me. Print it and we'll both sign it." She stepped back and crossed her arms over her chest, pushing up her boobs enough to make me drool.

Loki unfolded himself from his seat and the hair on the back of my neck stood up. He could be as slippery as an eel and as fierce as a viper. I'd seen him do shit that made me wonder who the fuck I'd taken up with, but when he defended what he considered his, he never let up.

I resisted the urge to protect Oriana as he strode up to her, producing a needle from somewhere. Again, his gaze slid to mine and his half-smile grew into a full-on smirk as he walked around her and held up the needle.

"I'm ready when you are, *ja*?"

Oriana frowned. "What's that for?"

"For this." He pricked his index finger with the needle and squeezed until blood welled up. He grinned at her gasp as he pressed his bleeding finger against the paper, writing his name with a flourish. "Now you."

"You want me to sign the contract in blood?" Her eyes widened and she swallowed hard.

Loki nodded, his eyes sparkling with insanity. "Best way to sign a contract. That way no one's confused and it can't be faked. DNA tells all, *ja*?"

Oriana let her gaze slide around the room, meeting a few eyes until she got to mine, but she refocused on the contract. "Give me a clean needle."

Damn, this woman is badass.

A new needle showed up and she took a deep breath before poking her finger. She grimaced as she forced the blood out of the hole then pressed her finger to the paper, signing some red squiggles. A weird ripple fluttered through the air, radiating from the paper they'd both signed. I watched it move and shot a look at Schnoz. Had he seen the freaky air movement?

Sometimes the man was a fuckin' sphinx, but he gave me a quick nod before returning his gaze to the major players as Neo handed Oriana a bandage for her finger.

"So are we good?" Loki asked as he stopped in front of his chair again.

"We're good. What now?"

"Now we show you to your...quarters." His gaze shot to me. "Scott, take Ms. Hunter to cabin number eight."

"Eight?" I raised my eyebrows as one of our biker chick members, Viper, brought me the key with one of her secret smiles. "But that's—"

"Ms. Hunter's new digs. Hook her up, Scott." Loki's eyes turned brittle and I decided to keep my mouth shut.

"Right. Come on, Numbers. Let's get you settled."

She raised an eyebrow. "Numbers?"

"Yeah." I escorted toward the door of the club house, half the guys watching me go with envy. "That's what you're here for, right? To work the numbers. Seems like a good nickname."

"I told you. I don't need a pet name because I'm not your pet."

That's what you think. But I kept the thought to myself as she paused at the door to the infirmary where Melrose sat drinking some sort of energy drink. Oriana crossed her arms over her chest.

"Congratulations. You got me stuck here, Melinda. Or is it really Melrose? Looks like lies are your thing." Venom filled her voice and anger crackled in the air.

Mel blanched, but shrugged as if it meant nothing. "It worked, didn't it? Don't worry, it won't be that bad, you'll see. Which cabin did they give you?"

"Eight," I said.

Mel's eyes widened. "But that's my cabin."

"Not anymore. I signed a contract. It's mine now." Oriana tilted her head. "Payback's a bitch, girlfriend."

I swallowed hard. The ice in her voice as she strode away could've frozen my balls. *Note to self: don't betray Numbers.* I raised my eyebrows at Melrose as her face crumpled, tears sliding down her cheeks. I'd watched her manipulate others with that tactic, but I didn't think it would work on Oriana. Mel had just nuked the bridge between them.

I caught up to Oriana just in time to hold the door open for her. See? I can be a gentleman when I want to. She sailed through like a queen and I couldn't help but admire her poise. She'd been abducted and told she couldn't leave unless she worked for the Concrete Angels, notorious motorcycle club of the Rockies. But instead of having a flailing tantrum, she'd turned the tables on us.

Wasn't bad for me either, since Loki had given her cabin number eight. I lived in cabin number nine.

"Wait up. Let me show you where you'll be staying." As much as I loved looking at her ass in denim, I was supposed to be directing her.

"Look, Scott. I'm not stupid and I can read. The numbers are tacked on the front of the cabins. I can figure out which one's mine." She held out her hand. "I'll take the key now."

Oh, no way in hell. I wasn't gonna let this opportunity go without a fight.

"No way, not gonna happen." I shook my head and led the way toward our cabins. "Loki said to show you and that's what I'm gonna do. Going against Loki's orders isn't smart, and I ain't stupid either."

I showed her to the two cabins set away from the rest by a good twenty feet because of a stubborn Ponderosa giant who'd gotten there first. Good thing was it provided shade when the summer got hot and I didn't mind a bit. Sometimes the sap was a bitch to get off the windows and I'd never park my bike near it, but when the bark heated up it smelled like a frickin' vanilla candle and the shade made a difference.

"I'll just make sure you're settled in." Hell, I'd like her to be settled in between my legs, but I also didn't want to lose my chance with her.

She snorted but followed me under the shade of the Ponderosa to the door of cabin eight. I opened the door for her but kept the key until she inspected the inside. She narrowed her eyes at me as she stepped over the threshold and scanned the room.

This had been our "guest cottage" for any members' long-term friends. For the last few months it'd belonged to Melrose, Roy's main squeeze.

"I need a packing tote." Oriana stood with her hands on her hips, her back to the door.

"What?" *Intelligent response, jackass.*

"I need a packing tote. I need to get rid of Mel's crap. I'm sure she'll want it wherever she ends up."

She waved at the knickknacks on every flat surface in the cabin. Even the kitchenette and bathroom had something cutesy and feminine. And pink. It looked like a Japanese anime had exploded everywhere with kitties and bows.

"Yeah, okay. You want help clearing it all out?"

Oriana paused, considering. She eyed me before trailing her gaze over the frou-frou contents in the cabin. A grimace followed. I didn't blame her. This place would've given me hives.

"Yeah, okay. Thanks."

Hot damn! I shoved the key in my pocket and ducked out of the cabin to wave at one of the Scooters loitering around the clubhouse entrance. Scooters were what we called the "probationary members" because they were the youngest and least experienced of the recruits. I had my doubts about some of them making it to full members—too much wanna and not enough be—but they were useful as gophers and cleaning crew.

"Yo, Scooter. C'mere." A gangly, pimple-faced punk with peach fuzz on his chin galloped over. "I need two or three sturdy boxes taped up and ready to go. Check behind the kitchen. Now."

"Yessir." He bobbed his head and did an about-face, scuttling off toward the clubhouse.

I stepped back inside and stopped dead. Oriana stood with her back to me, her shoulders hunched and shaking as sobs tore through her body. It was obviously a private moment not meant to be witnessed, but damn if it didn't rip something in my chest.

I'd seen women cry lots of times. Some did it to manipulate guys like me into fighting their battles for them. Others had been scared out of their minds, expecting us big, bad bikers to drag them into a back alley and rape them before selling into the sex trade. Loki didn't allow sex trafficking, but we didn't do much to disabuse anyone of the notion. Reputation, and all.

But watching Oriana, a woman of strength, cry when no one could see her broke open the only white knight tendency I possessed and made me want to roar a battle cry. I'd slay all her dragons and exorcise her demons just to make sure her smile and fire returned. I almost wrapped her in my arms for comfort, but I gritted my teeth and stepped back out the door to give her the privacy she thought she had.

"Fuck!" I stood beneath the Ponderosa and inhaled the vanilla candle scent like a yoga student doing Pranayama, that yogic breathing thing. It killed me not to do anything for Oriana, but I let the sweet spicy smell calm me down so I didn't deck the probie when he returned with the boxes. "Thanks."

I straightened my shoulders and headed for the door, making as much noise as possible so Oriana could preserve her cloak of cool before I showed up again. I knew all about saving face and putting up a good front of toughness in this outfit. She didn't want to be here and she'd been manipulated into it, but she'd make the best of it and kickass while she was at it, I was sure.

Once I stepped inside, Oriana stood tall and serene as if nothing really bothered her. So her eyes were a little red, but not so anyone would notice.

"I got you three boxes. Think that'll be enough to de-pink this place?"

She snorted and a small smile curled her sexy lips. "I'm not sure anything short of a good bonfire would fix it, but three boxes is a start."

In the end, it only took two boxes full of cutsie pink and white kitty shit to return the cabin to its usual cream, brown, and terra cotta (my aunt was a huge Georgia O'Keefe fan—sue me). We both breathed a sigh of relief at the same time and I grinned at her in momentary camaraderie.

"Better?" I set one of the boxes by the door.

"Much. I don't feel so girly anymore." She nodded as she settled into a chair at the little dinette table beside the window. "Now I can get some serious work done and hopefully solve your money issues in a few days. You can give Mel her crap and she can load the place back up again."

"You know, I don't think you're the girly type." I leaned against the wall separating the bedroom from the rest of the living space. "Which is good because I'm not into girly women."

And just like that, the camaraderie splintered into bright shiny pieces only to wink out of existence.

"Thanks for the four-one-one, Dr. Phil. I'm not here for your entertainment." She met my gaze with flames of anger burning beneath her golden irises.

"Whatever you say, Numbers. Need anything else while I'm here?"

"Yeah. I need my key and privacy."

She held out her hand and damn if I didn't feel like the queen required me to kiss her ring and swear fealty. I dug the key out of my pocket and brought it to her, stopping in front of her. She stared up at me without flinching, her expression expectant. I placed the key in her palm then flipped it over and brought her hand to my lips, kissing the knuckles. She gasped in surprise and color made her cheekbones rosy.

"Your key, milady. Chow's served in the clubhouse starting at six. I'll save a place for you." I released her hand and winked before sauntering to the door. I picked up the boxes and left the cabin without a backwards look, but I could feel her eyes burning into my back the whole way out.

****

Oriana

Thank goodness he's gone.

I'd never be able to get anything done with Scott hanging around my cabin. Shit, it had been bad enough when he helped me clear out the cartoonish kitty with a pink bow crap. He smelled like sun-warmed leather and a fresh-scented shampoo they only sell to men, but the marketing worked because I was hooked.

I sighed and scrubbed my face with my hands. At least he hadn't seen me break down. Contrary to popular belief, crying wasn't a sign of weakness, but a release valve for me. If I didn't cry, I'd pull someone's automatic pistol and go postal on their asses. Not very conducive to survival or my contractual obligation. *But it would feel great.*

Yeah, I didn't need help from the little devil on my shoulder.

I sighed and carried my bag into the bedroom, checking to be sure the bed had clean linens. It was made, but given how much cutsie kitty crap there'd been, I didn't trust it. I stripped the bed and carried the bedding plus the towels from the bathroom out to the main room. They needed to be washed before I used them.

But I had no idea how they got cleaned. Did the members of the Concrete Angels have a laundry service or maids? Or did they do their own? Was it a central laundry room or did each cabin have facilities?

"Shit."

"Shit goes in the toilet. That looks like laundry." The snarky feminine voice made me raise my gaze to a woman leaning against the doorjamb of my cabin.

"Nothing gets past you." I eyed the dark-haired woman wearing thigh-length cut-offs and an old Iron Maiden T-shirt. "Are there facilities to do our own laundry or is there a service?"

My visitor smirked, tossing her ponytail over her shoulder. "Wow, you really are a city girl, aren't you?"

I shot her a flat look. "Nope, just trying to figure out how you do things around here. I'm afraid when I was manipulated and abducted out here, I missed the orientation."

She pushed a loose strand of hair behind her ear and shrugged. "Yeah, I can see how that might make things tough. Good news is there's a laundry room on the north side of the clubhouse where we all do our stuff. Communal soap and machines, but individual elbow grease."

"Thanks."

I started to move past her when she shot out an arm with a red bandana wrapped around her wrist like a thick bracelet.

"Scuttlebutt is you caught the eye of my brother Scott." Her dark eyes glittered as the humor left them. "Word to the wise. Don't hurt him or you'll answer to me."

Anger surged and I raised my chin despite her shorter stature. "Listen up so there's no confusion. His broken heart isn't my responsibility. I didn't come here to hook up with anyone or lead anyone on or fuck anyone. In fact, I didn't want to come here at all. His lust is his problem. So back the fuck off."

"Oh, I can see why he likes you."

"Oh for glory's sake." I shook my head and pushed past her out the door. "Out. I need to lock up because I don't trust any of you."

"Aw come on." The woman slid past me as I shut the door behind her. "You don't trust a pack of Concrete Angels members when you're livin' with them?"

"Not any farther than I could comfortably spit out a dead sewer rat." I locked the door and pocketed the key.

She threw back her head and laughed a surprisingly sultry laugh. "Oh, I like you a lot, Numbers." She held out her hand. "Dollhouse."

"What?"

"My name's Dollhouse."

Out of habit, I took her hand and shook. "Nice to meet you." What the hell was I saying? It wasn't nice to meet any of these people.

"Let me help you with that." She took an armload of towels and wrinkled her nose. "Damn. How much perfume did Melrose use anyway? Gah."

Despite my unease with Dollhouse, I laughed. "I dunno. It kinda reminds me of old ladies who've lost their sense of smell."

"Yeah, totally. We have to wash these like yesterday." She hurried to the northern end of the clubhouse, past the gawking junior members of the Concrete Angels who lounged around until someone gave them something to do. A few of them eyed us with the typical male look of appraisal and my gut told me it wouldn't be long before one of them was stupid enough to make a move on her, me, or both.

Like the rest of the compound, the laundry room was neat, tidy, and painted. While the floor was concrete, it had been sealed with resin to make it shiny and easy to clean. We staggered inside under our loads and threw them into separate washers. Dollhouse handed me the soap and we started the machines.

"Why Dollhouse?" I leaned my back against the washer.

She smirked. "Because I can be anyone I want to be."

"Why not 'Chameleon' or something like that?"

Dollhouse shrugged. "Too many syllables for the boys to keep track of. You know how you have to help them."

I snorted. "Ain't that the truth."

"Also when I started in the Concrete Angels, I was workin' in a brothel north of Vegas called Last Dollhouse." She waved her hand at my look of dismay. "It wasn't that bad. I had dental and medical coverage, and the johns knew if they fucked with me, management would kick their asses and throw them out. Most of them were truckers who hadn't seen their old ladies in too long so I often played the part of the woman they missed."

"Wasn't fucking you what they paid for?" I asked dryly.

"Funny." She rolled her eyes. "It wasn't too bad. But when Loki stopped by on his way to wherever, one of his guys got a little stupid and gave me this scar." She turned and I followed her finger as it traced a thick scar from her collar bone over her shoulder.

"Holy shit."

"Yeah. Not pretty and therefore, not able to work in that field any longer. Loki made up for it, though. He gave me the asshole's place in the Concrete Angels and traded in his honkin' Harley for something a little more feminine." She winked. "I've been here ever since. No one fucks with me unless I say it's okay and the money's better, too." She checked the time on the washers. "Come on. Let's go talk to Neo about your internet access and shit like that. The stuff will be okay here."

I followed her back outside and sure enough, the young pups of the gang had converged on our path, waiting for us to show. Some of them were nearly half my age, but I suspected that wouldn't stop their raging hormones and egos.

We'd made it almost to the side door when one particularly short and robust punk moved in for a tête-a-tête.

"Hey, sugar, what's a pretty thing like you doing here?"

Aw hell. I'm way too sober for this shit.

I waited a few heartbeats for Dollhouse to step in and warn him off, but she seemed to be waiting to see what I'd do.

"Let's just stop that right there, all right?" I held up my hand as I looked down at him. I must have had at least six inches on him. "I'm not your sugar or a thing. If you have to address me, you can use the name Hunter. As for what I'm doing here? Working."

That was the wrong thing to say because his eyes flared with lust and he licked his lips. "What kind of work does a pretty thing like you do? Something...horizontal?"

"No, and no, I'm not interested in you. Leave me alone." I shifted to move around him and he reached out to grab my arm.

"Now don't be like that. You look like fair game to me. You're not wearin' someone's patch and the only girls who come here are fresh cunts."

I clenched my teeth so hard my jaw ached. There were so many things wrong with what he'd said that I couldn't begin to tamp down the rage rising inside me. I didn't belong to anyone. I wasn't a 'fresh cunt' for him to enjoy, and I wasn't a prostitute. At least not the sexual variety. I definitely sold my services for money, but they didn't involve sex with men.

"Take your hand off me before I cut it off." I purposely left my voice low and cold as I met his gaze. "If I have to resort to violence, not only will you be physically hurt, but you'll have to deal with Loki because my contract specifically said if someone sexually harasses me, I get to leave without repercussions. We both signed in blood. You wanna face him after that?"

"Hey, I'm not sexually harassing you. I'm just bein' friendly." He still hadn't released me.

I pointedly looked down at his hand and back up to him. "That's not friendly. Take your hand off me."

"Oh, come on, sweet thing. You know you want it."

"Oh, shit, Scooter, you didn't just—" Dollhouse took a step forward.

I'd had enough. My day had started out as shit and gotten progressively worse. I was done.

I clamped my free hand onto his where he grasped my arm and squeezed until the bones of his hand ground together. He yelped as I twisted out from under his grip and spun, slamming my elbow into the side of his head. He grunted and fell. I followed him down, yanking his arm behind him until he landed on his face with my knee in his back.

"When I fuckin' want anything from you, Scooter, I'll be sure to call with my dog whistle. In the meantime, if you fuckin' touch me again, I'll cut off your dick and feed it to you with ketchup." I pressed my knee to into his back. "Are we clear?"

He coughed but didn't answer.

I pulled his arm up at an acute angle. "Are we clear, Scooter?"

"Fuck yeah, we're clear. Fuckin' A."

I climbed off him and released his arm before stepping away. Dollhouse stood beside me as the young punk scrambled to his feet and slunk away, nursing his hand. I scowled and shook my head. Stupid boys. They all had to be taught again and again that women weren't their playthings. But some jackass kept pulling out the old sexist playbook and made our jobs that much harder.

"Nice moves, Numbers. Where'd you learn to fight like that?" Dollhouse sounded suitably impressed.

I didn't think they'd appreciate knowing a former FBI agent walked among them so I shrugged and winked. "CIA."

She laughed as I hoped and punched my shoulder. "Right. Come on. You deserve a drink after that stunt."

I nodded, though I wouldn't be drinking here. That seemed like a recipe for disaster given the angry little boy I'd pissed off. I sighed. I probably should've been more diplomatic, but I hadn't been feeling very charitable. And boys had to be held accountable for their shit.

We made it into the clubhouse without further incident and Dollhouse led me over to the bar. A woman with a cloud of soft-looking curls tied atop her head with scarf deftly held court behind the bar. Her dark eyes scanned me before she turned them on Dollhouse.

"What's up, Doll? Did I hear a rumor you kicked the shit outta one of the Scooters just now?"

Dollhouse shook her head. "Nope. Wasn't me. One of them got handsy with Numbers here and she put him down like a sick dog. It was beautiful."

The bartender smirked. "Nice." She held out her hand. "Karma."

"Hunter." I took her hand and shook it.

"Numbers Hunter, good handle. Fits you pretty well, too. What can I get you ladies to drink?" Karma settled her hands on the bar with a satisfied smile.

"Fat Tire for me." Dollhouse leaned against the bar counter as Karma popped the cap off a beer bottle. "What about you, Numbers?"

"Got anything non-alcoholic, but not too sugary?" I wasn't about to let my guard down around the wolves.

Karma raised an eyebrow. "Yeah, we got milk and lemonade. Want a straw with it?"

"You always this judgmental to someone who doesn't

want to get tipsy at lunchtime?" I countered with my own raised eyebrow.

Karma snorted. "Touché. Sure you don't want to drink like the big boys?"

"I don't drink with boys. I'd rather drink with women who know their shit. Lemonade please."

For all her snarky remarks, Karma pulled out a bottle of hoity-toity expensive lemonade only found at places like Whole Foods. *Someone has high end tastes.*

"Thanks."

"Please say you aren't one of those teetotalers." Dollhouse shot me a flat look.

"Nope, I just live by an old family motto. Don't drink if you have to think." I sipped the bottle. "Loki hired me to think, not to drink."

"But five o'clock arrives eventually, right?" Karma dipped her chin and raised both eyebrows.

I snorted. "Like y'all keep regular business hours."

"She's got a point, Karma." Dollhouse laughed as she raised her beer in tribute. "Hey, have you seen Neo around? We gotta get her set up on the internet."

"Yeah, I think he's in the Black Room." Karma nodded and pointed toward back of the clubhouse.

"Great. Thanks." Dollhouse took her beer and nodded at me to follow her.

"Black Room?" I caught up to her and raised my eyebrows. "What the hell is that?"

She shrugged. "It's our security and IT room. It's dark in there like a cave so he can see all the monitors, so we call it the Black Room."

I shuddered. "You'd have to be insane to stay in there all the time."

Dollhouse nodded as she paused at a wood door with old fashioned hinges spanning half the width. "You aren't insane, but I think Neo might be." And she knocked.

The bolt clicked from inside and she pushed the door

open with a nod. I followed with a shiver. I didn't really want to get stuck in the cave with an insane, stoic computer wiz. I stopped beside the door and left my foot between it and the doorjamb. There was no way I'd let it close.

"Hey, Neo. You got a special login for Numbers? She needs to get onto the network asap." Dollhouse sidled up beside him and ran her hands over his shoulders.

"I've asked you before, Doll. Please don't touch me while I'm typing." Neo's voice came out calm and smooth.

"Oh, you know you love it." She leaned down and kissed his head above the ear. "But I'll do as you ask this time because Numbers needs her stuff. But next time…" She wiggled her ass and winked at me.

"Did you bring your laptop or phone with you?" Neo's enigmatic gaze bored into mine.

"No, I was doing laundry." I shook my head. "Write down the network key and I'll get my laptop and phone hooked up."

He shot me a flat look. "Nice try, Numbers. Loki might trust you as far as the contract is concerned, but I don't. I'll make sure your laptop is connected. But no internet connection. Can't have you leaking our docs to the FBI."

I clenched my jaw and swallowed hard, hoping he couldn't see my face clearly enough in the darkness of the room. *Holy shit, does he know I'm former FBI?* I shrugged as he rose, staring at me with those enigmatic eyes.

"Whatever. You can come to my cabin and set me up there if you want. But the sooner you set up my connection to your servers and files, the sooner I can get this job done and leave all y'all alone." I hoped I sounded disinterested enough to keep him from looking too deeply into my background.

Though if Loki had required Mel to convince me to come to the compound, he had to know I'd been with the FBI until just over two years ago doing forensic accounting on corporations with too many offshore accounts. The current POTUS's accounts had been a definite concern and I'd found things I still couldn't talk about.

But I had to get out of that room. That darkness combined with the blue light of the monitors made my skin crawl and brought up too many memories of being alone in the Denver offices of the FBI at night. I'd felt so invincible as a seasoned agent. Someone who had the training and the skills to take care of herself.

But, as the saying goes, there's always someone better at what you do, and there's always someone worse. That night, I'd been the 'worse.'

I shoved the memories away and hoped the sweat on my forehead would be mistaken for the heat resting on the world outside. *Fuck, why won't those damn memories leave me alone?* I'd gone to therapy. I'd made my statements and presented my evidence. I even left the FBI so I wouldn't have to see my attacker again. But it didn't matter to the memories. They still kept sneaking up on me when I least expected it.

I swallowed hard as the smells of his breath and his cologne filled my nose, and suddenly I was back in that broom closet, nowhere to run, my training useless. I tried to scream, to make as much noise as possible so the friendly rent-a-cop who made his rounds would find me and stop this. But my throat closed over the sound as solidly as the rag he stuffed into my mouth and I could only wheeze.

Panic rose with the voices, but none of them made any sense. The heat and weight of his body against me smothered everything until I was left in the wailing darkness of hot threats and painful intrusion. Held down, beaten, and…and…

"Numbers! Hey, come on. Look at me. Numbers. Oriana."

Numbers. Oriana. Those were names I once possessed. No, Oriana was my name. Numbers was new, a handle given to me by a cocky biker with seafoam-green eyes and broad shoulders.

"Come on, Oriana. Come back to me. You're safe."

The gravelly voice sounded full of reassurance and concern. No one had ever spoken to me with the same quality of voice. No one had ever cared enough since I'd left home. Most hadn't thought I'd make it through the FBI's training, including my instructors. I was too tall, too willowy, to blonde. But this voice was different. Stronger, encouraging without being patronizing, masculine without being assholian.

"Open those eyes for me, now. Come on, swe— Numbers."

I opened my eyes to stare up at Scott crouched over me. The ceiling rose above him and I realized it had very elegant baroque cornices. Movement had me taking in the other faces around us: Dollhouse, Karma, Neo, Michael, and another man who reminded me of the crazy goalkeeper in a British prison soccer movie I'd once seen. None of these people had been in Denver when I worked at the FBI, which meant I was no longer in the broom closet with…with *him.*

"Let me up." I struggled to get to my feet, shame burning through me. *Nothing like showing my weakness to the only people who'd take advantage of it.*

All I wanted to do was crawl into a hole and never come out again. I thought my therapy had worked, that I could function as a normal human being now. But I was dead wrong. I shook my head to hold back my tears. *Can't cry in front of them.* I gritted my teeth and swallowed hard as I straightened my shoulders.

Never let them see you sweat. I strode out of the clubhouse and straight to my cabin without another look behind me. I had to get somewhere safe where I could regroup. Maybe only Neo would come to set up the computer into the network and I'd never have to leave my cabin again. I'd get the work done, safe within the pathways and puzzles of numbers, show Loki and the rest of the Concrete Angels where their money had gone, and leave them in the dust. They'd become another event in my past like my time at the FBI. And I'd remain broken but safe.

I fumbled with the key to my cabin but managed to get the door open on the third try. Perfumed cool air hit me in the face and the annoyance broke some of my control. I sobbed at the unfairness of it all—Mel's lies and abduction, the blood contract, the Scooter's sexual harassment, public panic attack, and the stench of Mel's perfume—but the tears didn't start until I'd shut the door behind me.

I hurried to the bedroom and closed that door as well. Then I slid down the wall and wrapped my arms around my upraised knees, sobbing my heart out.

CHAPTER THREE

Scott

"What the hell happened?" I didn't mean to roar, but
watching Oriana turn into a blanked-out zombie who
slithered into a dead drop scared the living shit out of me.

"I don't know, Scott." Dollhouse wore concern and
bewilderment like a matched set of earrings. "One minute
we were talking to Neo about getting her hooked up to the
network and the next she backed out of the room and
crumpled to the floor with that blank look on her face. We
didn't do or say anything to her. Right, Neo?"

The computer geek nodded, wearing a look of
confusion for the first time since I'd known him.
"Seriously, Scott. We didn't do anything to her."

"Then what the hell happened? Why was she like that?
Something must have triggered it."

I'd seen reactions like Oriana's before in people who'd
seen combat or some sort of trauma. Post-Traumatic Stress
Disorder they called it now. I'd served my mandatory four
years in the military (my father's requirement) and I'd seen
it in the soldiers coming back from places like Afghanistan

and Iraq. I'd done my time and gotten the hell out, but some experiences weren't easily forgotten, and many of my buddies hadn't been the same.

"She was in the Black Room?" I didn't know her background beyond being a forensic accountant, but maybe something had happened to her.

"Yeah."

"Was it locked or latched?"

Dollhouse shook her head. "Nope. Something propped it open while we were there."

Fuck. What had happened to set her off? "I'm gonna go talk to her."

"Scott."

Aw shit, I knew that tone of voice from Schnoz. I stopped and looked back at Michael. "What?"

"Let me go talk to her." He shrugged out of his leather cut and draped it over a chair. "She doesn't trust any of us and if we go in there hot, she might lock us out for good. All right?"

I wanted to argue I was the best man for the job, but Michael had this weird way of making everyone feel comfortable, safe, and heard even if they'd just met him. *It's gotta be the British accent.* What was it with American women and accents originating in the UK?

"Yeah, fine. But keep your hands to yourself." I tried to hold back my urge to kill him.

"Scout's Honor. Am I right thinking she's suffering some form of PTSD?" Michael turned to Karma and waved toward the coffee maker. "Got any chamomile tea back there?"

"Yeah, comin' up." Karma ducked away.

Michael turned back to me. "I'll get her to open up, Scott. We'll find out what's wrong, okay? It'll be fine, mate."

I wished I could take his word for it. To be honest, he was usually right. But I'd seen the look of hopelessness on

Oriana's face. It was the same look I'd seen on abused children and battered women. Defeat and resignation. A woman that strong and smart should never have those emotions stamped into her.

Karma brought the tea on an honest-to-glory silver tray, with cream and sugar in silver servers and matching silver spoons. I raised my eyebrows at her and she shrugged.

"It's for special occasions. Sometimes you have to break out the big guns and show a little class."

"Where did you find a silver tea service?" They were even polished to a high gleam.

She winked. "Estate sale."

Michael picked up the tray and headed for the door. "I'll find out what's wrong and get it sorted. Don't worry."

"Yeah, right." I shook my head, trying to figure out what to do while Michael worked his magic. "Hey, Neo. You can look up people's backgrounds, right?"

He snorted. "Is that a trick question?"

"Yeah, yeah, smartass. What about Oriana Hunter's background?" I followed him back toward his lair in the Black Room.

"Already done."

"What?" I gaped at him. "When?"

"When Melrose first told Loki about her. He insisted we knew who we were letting look at our records." Neo stepped into the darkness and I followed.

"So what did you find out?" Maybe it would give me a leg-up on hooking up with Oriana without breaching her contract.

"Not much beyond her being former FBI."

"What? Are you serious?"

"As a heart attack." He held up a manila folder full of papers but didn't let it go. "Are you sure you want to look at that?

I frowned. "Yeah, why?"

"Most women don't like you checking up on them. They're prefer to tell you their stuff themselves. If Ms. Hunter finds out you've been digging through her records, it might blow your one shot with her." He still held the folder.

"What the fuck do you know about it?" I narrowed my eyes. What was in her file?

Neo shrugged. "Call it speaking from bitter experience." He pulled the folder back. "Listen, I had to look this stuff up for Loki to make sure she wasn't a competitor's moneyman, but that means I know things she might not want the general population knowing."

Unease squeezed my gut. "Like what?"

Neo shook his head. "Tell you what. I'll keep this folder with me. Let's see if Schnoz can get her to open up and talk about it. If she does, you'll have an idea of how to approach her. If she doesn't, I'll let you take a look and you can decide what to do then. Okay?"

I hated being in the dark. I'd worked too damn hard to get where I was in Loki's organization, but Neo was right about Oriana. She struck me as a woman who had her secrets and they might be uglier than we all guessed. Neo knew and he wasn't talking for now. Hopefully Michael would get Oriana to trust him and he'd pave the way to my getting in there.

But if not, there was always plan B. Once I figured out what that was.

In the meantime, I needed to check on our distributors and distribution routes up north into Canada to be sure the money Numbers would be checking kept flowing. Between the import of prescription drugs and the export of designer accessories like shoes, purses, and electronics, we made a killing and then some. I didn't really want to focus on business and commerce, but it would force me to give Schnoz some time to get Oriana to open up.

And to figure out Plan B if it doesn't work.

Yeah, it had better work.

****

Oriana

I'm not sure how long I sat there crying my eyes out, but eventually the tears slowed and I was able to catch my breath from the sobbing. The compound had grown quiet after my retreat and no one seemed interested in checking out the emotional female. *Thank goodness.* I didn't want company and I certainly didn't want to see them with my face a blotchy mess.

Rubbing my eyes to wipe away the last of the tears, I steadied my breathing and squared my shoulders. I needed to make this cabin my own. It would've been nice to hose down the inside, but I'd have to rely on the breeze coming through the windows to air out the perfumed stench.

One step at a time.

That had been my mantra after the assault. I couldn't handle the whole day, but the time could be broken up into little manageable chunks. I could do increments, like an integral in mathematics. Little units of measurement added up to create a whole. I could do that.

Taking a deep breath, I pushed to my feet and opened the bedroom door. The living room of the cabin remained as I'd left it with my laptop on the table. I shot a look at the kitchenette and wondered if there might be some tea in the cupboards. There was a kettle on the stove at least.

I took one step and someone knocked on the door. My first instinct was to drop and scramble back into the bedroom, but I gritted my teeth and closed my eyes, willing my heartbeat to steady. *It'll be okay. They won't hurt me.* Or at least they wouldn't hurt me physically. *Words and innuendos work just as well. Like at the FBI.*

I shook my head as the knock sounded again. *Just*

answer it and get it over with. I strode to the door and checked the peep hole. *What the?* Grasping the knob, I pulled the door open.

"Hey, Ms. Hunter. I just wanted to check on you. May I come in?" Michael's rich British accent slid over me and soothed some of my jangled nerves.

Don't fall for it. It's a trick.

I shook my head. "I'm fine."

He held up a real silver tea service on a tray and I blinked. "I have some tea to share if you're interested. I thought it would help. Please?"

I narrowed my eyes. "Why?"

He tilted his head, compassion rolling off him like a balm. "Because it didn't take a genius to see you were very upset and suffering effects from some trauma."

"Who told you that?" Oh fuck, had they gotten a hold of my file?

"You did." He nodded to the tea. "I'll just leave the tea and if you don't want to talk about it, that's fine. We can talk about anything you like. I just wanted to make sure you're okay."

Before I could stop him, he'd stepped through the doorway and headed for the table. I squawked in protest and turned with him, and for just a moment I could've sworn I saw a huge set of silver-black wings folded on his back.

Wait, wings?

I blinked and the feathered appendages disappeared. Like they were never there. *Man, maybe I should drink the tea.* I closed the door and strode to his side until I could look into his face. Who was this guy? He smiled at me as he set out the tea cups—real crystal with sterling silver bases—and poured tea from the pot before handing one to me.

"Cream or sugar?"

I shook my head. "No. Why are you here?"

He pulled out one of the two chairs and settled into the second one. "Join me. I'm here because we're truly worried about you. What happened in the clubhouse? Did someone do something to you?"

"No."

I sat down and wrapped my hands around the tea. The heat seeped into my palms and some of the tension in my shoulders released. I wanted to close my eyes, but I couldn't let my guard down around this man. He might seem friendly, but so had Dirk at the FBI.

No, I'm not thinking about that.

"You know, when I first came to the Concrete Angels." He paused and snorted, rueful amusement curling his lips. "I didn't trust anyone either. They appeared to be an unruly bunch of heathens bent on threat and destruction. Especially Loki and his then second-in-command, my older brother Luke. But you'd be surprised at how much these people care about each other and look out for all their members. I was."

I snorted and shook my head. "I know what you're doing, Michael. Establish a rapport so the person you're trying to convince relaxes."

His smiled. "Is it working?"

"No. You're trying to sell me a load of horseshit. I've seen your Scooters and how they treat people, women in particular. I'm a pair of tits and a pussy to them. The only thing stopping them from raping me is my own defensive abilities and the contract I signed. And the only reason the contract stops them is because they're afraid of what Loki will do if they break it." I dropped my gaze to the tea in the cup. "No one cares about me but me."

He lifted his hand and extended his arm until I met his gaze again.

"If you touch me, I'll stab you with the knife I always carry on me."

He pulled his hand back and sipped his tea. "Good to

know. I guarantee if any of the Scooters touch you, they'll be dealt with."

"Uh-huh. Pretty words. But I know how the "Old Boys Club" works. Either they'll get a slap on the wrist or you'll warn me to be more careful." I shrugged. "Don't worry about it. I'll be gone in a few days and then it won't matter. You won't have to require them to change their behavior."

"You seem pretty convinced that's how the Concrete Angels work."

I barked an incredulous laugh. "I've lived it. Women live it every day, even when men deny that's what's going on because they can't see it. The Concrete Angels aren't different than any other organization run by men. Bros before women."

"I believe the phrase is 'bros before hos.'"

I scowled. "I know what the correct phrase is. I just don't think of myself as a whore. Go figure." I stood and pointed at the door. "Now get out."

"Please, Ms. Hunter. Let me help." He didn't move from the chair.

"Why?" I raised my chin and stared him down.

"Because you're hurting."

"Yes, I am hurting. I've been lied to, kidnapped, railroaded, and threatened. And now you come in here with a pot a tea and a smile and think I'll just bare my soul to you because you try to sweet talk me into believing you give a shit? Hate to burst your ego bubble, but I'm not your typical gullible bimbo."

"That's not the kind of hurting I was referring to." He met my gaze and despite my refusal to back down, he still seemed to see into my soul. "I'm talking about what happened in the clubhouse."

Fear spiked through me, but I shrugged. "What about it?"

For a moment, frustration filtered through his expression but it disappeared as he raised his eyebrows and spread his hands. "I can't help you if you won't talk to me."

"Why would you want to?" I raised my own eyebrows.

He tilted his head with a half-smile. "It's what I do. I'm empathic and when someone's hurting, I tend to move heaven and earth to help the pain stop."

I crossed my arms over my chest. To his credit, he didn't stare at my boobs. "Why should I trust you?"

"Because, like you, I live by my word and follow the rules. If I say I'm going to do something, I do it."

Damn, he looked so sincere. I wanted to believe him. Hell, I wanted to tell someone about the assault in the broom closet. Someone who'd believe me. But I'd learned the hard way that no one would.

They'd pointed out all the reasons I'd caused the assault and said it was my fault. Clothes, hair, perfume, being friendly. All were threats against the "innocent" men just minding their own business. They couldn't be blamed if they were tempted by a harlot wearing a business suit with her hair in a ponytail who offered a cordial smile to them every morning in the breakroom. She must have been parading around, offering herself like a tasty treat.

I didn't realize I was crying until Michael rose and took a couple of steps toward me. "Ms. Hunter."

"Don't. Don't touch me." I couldn't stop the tears but I could stop the contact.

"Please, come sit down again. Have some tea. It'll help even if I can't." He gestured to the chairs but didn't offer to touch me again. His mouth and shoulders tightened as if he wanted to gather me into his arms, but he stepped back and sat down. "Please, Oriana."

It was the first time he'd said my name, but the soothing quality of his voice made more of my resistance fade. I'd been carrying this secret around for two years and it'd grown unbearably heavy. I wanted to give it to someone else to carry, but no one had backed me up. I was the pariah and the one with nightmares, but everyone said it was my fault. More tears slid down my cheeks as I returned to my chair. He refilled my mug with warm tea and waited for me to say something.

"I'm so tired." I held my cup to anchor myself in reality, but reality sucked just the same as the past. "Tell me again why you want to help me? You've known me all of two hours."

Michael's lips curled into a sad smile. "It's what I do."

I nodded. "Right. You're in a notorious biker club and you help people. That's great. Tell you what. Why don't you take your vague responses right on outta here and I'll just get settled? Mmkay?" I was tired of carrying my secrets, but two could play the vague game.

"You carry a lot of anger around with you."

I barked an unhappy laugh. "Yup."

"You don't want to tell me the reason?" he asked.

"You don't want to admit why you're really here?" I countered.

"I don't think you'd believe me if I told you."

I nodded. "Fabulous. Thanks for the tea." I didn't have time for a game of 'guess my special talent' that men liked to play. "The door's that way."

He laughed, a delighted sound despite my rude dismissal. "You don't give any quarter, do you?" He shook his head, but his smile remained. "All right. Here's the truth. I've had a lot of experience with combat veterans and domestic violence victims, and I can recognize the signs of PTSD from violent trauma. You have a lot of them. Being brought against your will up to a motorcycle club's compound probably doesn't engender trust of your 'friend' and hosts.

"But I also recognize a soul desperately asking for help. My guess is you've been isolating yourself and hiding from life since the trauma you experienced." He held his tea cup up, the delicate crystal and silver appearing fragile in his big hands. "I can give you the help and recovery you've been seeking."

I snorted. "What, with drugs? I have a shrink for that."

He shook his head. "No, as someone who can listen to your story without criticism or disdain."

Glory, that one sentence damn near broke me.
Yearning hit my heart like a freight train and I wanted to blurt out everything that had happened, releasing the anger, pain, frustration, and hopelessness onto someone else's shoulders.

But could I trust Michael? Could I give him the ugliness that had been wearing me down for the last two years? I could barely eat or sleep, my friends and family had retreated, and I worked alone. *You're gonna have to trust someone sometime.* Yeah, but was it Michael?

Why not? He doesn't know me. Maybe it was better to hand it to a stranger rather than someone who had preconceived notions of who I was supposed to be.

"I don't know if I can tell you. I've been holding onto it for so long." I shook my head and closed my eyes as the tears flooded out of me. "It was at my previous job. I loved it there. I loved what I was doing. I thought I was helping people."

"In the FBI." It was a statement rather than a question.

"Yeah." It didn't surprise me he knew. I suspected Loki had a dossier on me, I just hoped it didn't include too much of my life. "Please don't tell the others. I don't need to be ostracized for that, too. It's my past, and I was damn good at it, but it's over now."

"Why did you leave the FBI if you loved it so much?"

"I couldn't stay. Something happened and I was blamed for it even if it wasn't my fault." It wasn't my fault, but my coworkers and family and friends didn't see it that way. "After a while I couldn't stand to be around the silent looks and the gossip."

"Who actually did the crime?"

"My supervisor, my boss. He—" I couldn't say the

words. They stuck in my throat so hard my voice came out in a low wail. My tears sent a fresh wave down my face. "No one believed me. They all talk a good game about reporting incidents, but when it's someone highly respected and decorated, they questioned my memory, my wardrobe, my professionalism. No one could believe such a high-ranking officer *of the law* would commit such an illegal act."

I raised my gaze to meet Michael's blue eyes full of compassion. "He did it to me, but he still has his job. He took more than my autonomy. He took my happiness, my strength, and my job away from me. He took it all. Oh glory, he took everything."

Sobs clobbered me for the second time that day and this time I let Michael gather me into his arms when he got up. I couldn't hold in the grief at the loss of so much. I'd been as strong as I could throughout the process of reporting my superior for rape, but in the end it had been too much for me to stay. Some of my coworkers had pitied me. Others openly disbelieved my story. But the memories of that dark place with my hands cuffed behind my back were etched in my memory, eating away at my sanity one black moment at a time.

Michael let me sob away against his chest, his strong arms holding me as he murmured soothing nonsense into my hair. It felt so good to be held against another human being, not in a sexual way, but with comfort and compassion. I clung to him with the determination I used to have before the rape and the sharp edges of my agony wore down in the face of his empathy. *He's using emotional sandpaper*. The idea made me smile.

It's called love, you idiot. I lost my smile but didn't doubt the thought. I hadn't been loved by anyone in a long time, including myself, but Michael offered it without reservation. I opened my eyes and found myself encased not only in his arms, but silver-black feathers. I must have jerked as I blinked because when I looked again, they were gone and only his arms remained around me.

I raised my head and met his gaze, blinking owlishly.

"Feeling better?" He didn't smile, but the question didn't feel hostile.

Surprisingly, yes, I was. Better and lighter. At least until the door to my cabin opened and Scott stepped inside. He growled and slammed the door behind him.

"What the fuck is going on here?"

CHAPTER FOUR

Scott

Schnoz promised! He promised he wouldn't do
anything to snag Oriana's attention. But when I used the
master key to come into her cabin and found her wrapped
in his arms, gazing at him with adoration, I just about lost
my shit and my lunch.

"What the fuck is going on here?" The words were out
of my mouth before I took in Oriana's tear-stained face.

"Scott, you gave me your word you'd wait until I got
back."

"Why, so you could move in on my—"

"On *your* what, exactly?" Oriana's knife-edged gaze
slashed to mine. "I'm not *your* anything, Scott. And how
the fuck did you get in here? I didn't invite you. Get out."

Yeah, this wasn't exactly how I'd thought things
would go. I didn't like how close Schnoz had gotten to
Oriana, but I really didn't like her kicking me out and not
him.

"Oriana—"

"I said get out." She at least stepped out of Michael's

arms and headed for the kitchenette to rinse out the teacups.

Michael shot me a look and shrugged when I scowled at him. He nodded to the door with a look that said he'd follow me and I shook my head.

"Are you listening to me, Scott, or is your ego too big to hear through? Get. The. Fuck. Out."

I rolled my eyes but nodded. "Fine, I'm getting out. You better be comin' too, Schnoz."

"Yeah, yeah, I won't be a moment." Michael nodded, frustration filling his eyes.

I wasn't sure if he was pissed I caught him making moves in Oriana or if it was something else, but I would be happy to set him straight the moment he came outside. I left reluctantly but would wait for him under the Ponderosa to kick his ass. I scowled, seething, but the vanilla scent combined with the dry heat and pine calmed me down a little. I closed my eyes and took a deep breath.

Which whooshed out of me the moment Michael slammed me up against the trunk.

"What the fuck, Schnoz?"

"I should bloody well ask you the same thing!" He snarled at me, his huge nose in my face. I'd never seen him that angry and unease skittered through me. "I was *this* close to getting Oriana to open up, you stupid git. What were you thinking?"

"That you were making moves on her." I met his anger with my own.

"Oh for glory's sake. I gave you my word."

"Yeah, well, it looked like you weren't upholding your end of the deal there, asshole."

"I was comforting her, Scott." He rolled his eyes but didn't let me up from the tree. "She's had trauma, you wanker, and while she didn't say the word 'rape,' I'm pretty sure that's what it was."

"What?" That stopped me and my stomach sank. "Rape? You mean she's broken?"

"No, you asshole. Stop thinking with your dick for five minutes."

If I wasn't against the Ponderosa's trunk, he would've cuffed the back of my head.

"She's stronger than you or me, but sex isn't something she takes lightly. She has to trust her partner enough not to hurt her. So, when you do get to have sex with her, it'll be on her terms and with her on top."

"How do you know that? Did she tell you?" I was still trying to process the word 'rape.'

Michael sighed and shot a look around at the yard. It sat deserted. Even the Scooters had retreated inside from the afternoon's heat.

With one last look around, Michael leaned forward and closed his eyes, pressing his forehead against mine. I couldn't go anywhere with him holding me in place, so I closed my own eyes before I went cross-eyed. I'd never noticed Michael's scent, but for just a moment he smelled like the climbing jasmine flowers in my mother's serenity garden.

The vision that filled my head at his touch consisted of darkness and the musty smells of stored chemicals. Metal handcuffs cut into my wrists as my arms strained behind me. Panic and helplessness surged as I tried to scream around the rag stuffed into my mouth. Then pain flared lower down in my body, burning agony I couldn't stop.

I yanked my head away from Michael and met his sad blue eyes.

"What the fuck was that, Michael?" My voice came out shaky and panicked.

"That's a fraction of what Oriana experienced. I was trying to help her get through it." He released me and stepped back. "That's what she sees in her nightmares and every time she steps into a dark room."

"Like Neo's lair."

"Right. It triggered her."

"Holy fuck."

He nodded as he pointed at me. "So, for once you're gonna have to be a man more than a dick and woo her. Seriously, mate. She'll come to you for sex and comfort. But you'll have to listen to her and pay attention to her pleasure rather than yours. Think you can do that?"

I scowled. "Go to hell, asshole."

He laughed, though his eyes remained haunted and sad. "That's my brother Luke's purview." He clapped me on the shoulder. "Good luck, Scott."

"Hey, what am I supposed to do now?" I waved in the direction of Oriana's door, now firmly shut.

He shot a look toward the cabin and shrugged. "Wait, I guess."

His parting words made anger flare. I'd never been very good at waiting, but I'd already screwed up spending more time with her today. I swore and stomped off toward the workshop to work in my Harley. I didn't really work on it so much as clean it up and make sure it worked right, like field-stripping a rifle. There were mechanics in our crew to make sure our rides ran smooth, but I liked to keep track of my own bike.

The smells of oil, hot metal, and rubber hit my nose as I stepped into the relative cool shade. A couple of the other guys were hanging out in front of the fans as they tinkered with their own rides. Roy, Melrose's boyfriend, grumbled to himself as he worked. I couldn't hear much of what he said over the fan, but I caught a few words here and there.

"Stupid meddling bitch...FBI...Snooping...Fuck!" A socket wrench dropped to the concrete floor and skittered over to my feet. "Oh, hey, Scott. Can I have that back?"

Did Roy look guilty for a moment as held his hand out for the wrench?

"Everything okay, Roy?"

"Yeah, close enough." He scowled as he crouched by his ride again. "Woman troubles. Melrose turned into a sniveling bitch when Loki kicked her out of her cabin."

I didn't feel much sympathy for Mel since she'd pissed off Oriana. Not that I was surprised and I was damn glad she'd come to our compound, but Mel shouldn't have lied to her. The irony of my emotional response didn't escape me, but it didn't change how I felt.

"Can you believe she brought her pink, stinky shit into my place?" Roy scowled. "It smells like a damn perfume factory."

"Why are you with her, then? I mean, she's in your space now, man."

He snorted. "Free pussy. Why else?"

Yesterday, I would've agreed with him. I'd had my share of free pussy and hot tail. But after a while, some of that free pussy got clingy and wasn't so free anymore. Then it became less fun and a pain in the ass. I didn't want to make the effort to keep the women happy. *That could happen once you get a taste of Oriana.* The traitorous voice slipped into my thoughts, but I shoved it away. There was something different about Numbers and I wouldn't give up my opportunity to figure out what it was.

"Dude, there are easier ways of getting free pussy." I suspected Melrose wouldn't like Roy's assessment of her, but it wasn't my relationship. Maybe she liked getting treated like a convenient toy

"Maybe, but Mel's easy." Roy shrugged as he tightened something on his bike. "She works for me for now."

"Better you than me, brother." I shook my head as I tinkered with my own ride. "So you're gonna let her stay in your cabin?"

"Yeah, if she can stop blubbering all the time about losing her place. I swear, Loki did it just to see what Melrose would do."

I snorted. Roy wasn't wrong. That was Loki's MO. He poked the bear just to see how loud it would roar and how many people it'd kill. And he'd become more ornery now that someone embezzled some of our income, as if pissing off his crew released some of his frustration.

Hopefully Oriana can find the asshole soon so Loki doesn't come after me.

"More than likely." I nodded my head but didn't meet his gaze. I didn't want to tell him I was glad Melrose had to give up her cabin. Not that Oriana would be willing to spend time with me. *But the possibility's there.* "She staying with you here tonight?"

Roy shook his head. "Nah, I'm taking her down to Denver to make her feel better. I gotta check on some contacts and figured it'd cheer her up."

"That's nice of you." Surprisingly so.

"Yeah, well, she doesn't put out when she's upset, so I might as well get her in a better mood so I can get laid."

Oh. Right, it was mostly about him. While I thought him a jackass and a pig, I couldn't say I hadn't done the same over the years. I'd been in Loki's crew a long time and the pussy and money had flowed like a river. But I'd been single for a while now and no one had tempted me. I'd gotten bored with the hookups. Besides, I liked Oriana, her fire and her strength. I wanted to hook up with her, but I didn't want it to be a one-time-thing.

Not that she was speaking to me at the moment.

I turned my focus back to the bike. Michael said I'd have to wait. I wondered how long that'd be.

****

Oriana

I rubbed my face with my hands and sighed. I'd unpacked and cleaned the cabin as much as I was able, but I had nothing left to do except get my laundry and find something to eat. I didn't want to face anyone after my

55

PTSD episode, but more than likely everyone already knew what it was all about. Michael probably got big points for braving the wrath of the crazy woman to get the story.

Except Michael didn't seem like the kind of guy to blab secrets. He struck me as a man who had a great deal of wisdom and experience, and kept the secrets entrusted to him like a vault. I frowned and shook my head. What would a guy like that be doing in the Concrete Angels?

Stop stalling. I needed to get my laundry at least. And probably convince the computer gremlin to come connect my laptop to the network. *As long as I don't have to go into his lair.* Maybe I could send him an email. The last thought made a rueful laugh erupt and chased away some of the post-episode exhaustion.

Squaring my shoulders, I took a deep breath and reached for the doorknob just as someone knocked. I froze as my breath stalled in my chest. Panic surged and my hands tightened into fists. I clenched my teeth and dug my fingernails into my palms to remind myself I was safe. Maybe if I held still, the person on the other side would go away.

Seconds ticked by and I slowly relaxed, until they knocked again.

Aw fuck, just get it over with. It wouldn't get better the longer I waited.

I grasped the doorknob and twisted, breathing as slow as I could to keep myself calm.

To my surprise, two people waited on the doorstep. Dollhouse stood with my laundry dried and folded in her arms. Neo stood behind her, unease and chagrin gracing his features.

"Hey, Numbers. Mind if we come in? I brought your laundry and Neo says he can get you hooked up to the network." Dollhouse gave me a worried smile. "Would that be okay?"

"Uh, yeah. Okay." I stepped back as they marched

inside. "The laptop is on the table."

Neo nodded and headed for the computer. I suspected he dealt with computer and circuitry problems better than emotional ones. I could relate.

"Where do you want the laundry?" Dollhouse paused in the middle of the room.

"On the bed is fine. Thanks." I meant my gratitude. She'd saved me from having to return to the clubhouse and all the recriminating stares.

"You're hooked into the network and I've set up shortcuts on your desktop to the Concrete Angels' financial records." Neo stood in front of me, one hand on the back of his neck and his gaze on the floor. "I'm really sorry about the Black Room. If I'd known, I wouldn't have had you come in."

"Thanks, Neo. I appreciate it." I nodded and though his gaze was on the floor, some of the tension left his shoulders. "Next time I'll just email you."

He snorted, though he didn't smile, but I got the impression I'd amused him. "Yeah, good. I created a simple login for you. Username is Numbers and this is the password." He handed me a sticky note. "Change it to something you can remember as soon as you get in."

"So you won't know it?"

He smirked. "Oh, I'll know it, but no one else will. See you." He ducked out the front door as I laughed.

"That's a lot better sound." Dollhouse came back into the main room. "They're gonna start serving dinner here soon. Want me to bring you back a plate of the goods?"

Had this woman read my mind? I nodded, relief loosening all my muscles. "Yes, please, and thank you."

"Yeah, I figured after that dramatic exit, you didn't really want much company tonight."

I nodded again. "Can I ask you a question?"

"You mean, beyond that one?" She winked as I rolled my eyes. "Yeah, go ahead."

"Why are you helping me?"

She offered me a sad smile as she tilted her head. "Because having PTSD doesn't make you weak and I've been where you are." She shrugged. "And my brother likes you. So, yeah."

She waved as she sailed out the door and I stood there, trying to figure out what the hell had happened. *This whole day is fucked up.* First, I was manipulated and kidnapped. Then, I was coerced, sexually harassed, and triggered into a PTSD episode. And now someone was helping me with laundry and bringing me food. I tried to remember when a total stranger did something nice and couldn't come up with a single instance.

Shaking my head, I shuffled into the bedroom and dug out my toiletries for a shower. Sometimes the water pounding on my body recentered me after an episode and I could face the world again in a limited capacity. It also helped me turn my chattering brain off and reminded me how to feel instead of react.

I closed the blinds in the bedroom and stripped down to nothing. Damn, had I locked the front door? It took me a moment to remember this had been a motel with automatically locking doors. *Except Scott had gotten in without my key.* Which only meant he had a master or a copy. I debated engaging the security chain, but that meant I had to go out into the main room, naked. I shook my head and turned on the water in the shower. The water pressure appeared decent and I sighed when I stepped under the spray.

Perfect.

I turned off my brain long enough to wash and relax, the only thoughts flitting through concerned the pleasure in the heat of the water.

Scott could give me heated pleasure.

I jerked as if someone had thrown a bucket of ice on me and shut off the shower. I stood dripping in the bathtub as the last of the water draining out of the shower head. What the hell was I thinking? I didn't know if I was more surprised with the thought of pleasure with Scott or that I'd had thoughts of sex at all. Ever since I'd left the FBI, sexual interaction didn't show up on my radar.

But here I stood, wet from my shower, and the idea of his kisses warmed me from the inside out.

I'm insane.

That was debatable. I'd voluntarily agreed to work for one of the most notorious motorcycle clubs in the Rocky Mountains. My former employer would kill to get the same opportunity. They had killed to do it. *Shouldn't have stood by the rapist, then.* Of course, if they'd fired his ass, I wouldn't have been here to get the intel on the Concrete Angels. *Maybe.* I hadn't really wanted to stay after the rape.

I shook my head at my stupid musings and toweled dry. Someone would be bringing a meal soon and I didn't really want to meet them in my full, naked glory, towel or not. I returned to my bedroom and sifted through the clothes Mel had selected for me. She'd picked mostly jeans, my more sensual blouses, and a couple pairs of shorts. Thank goodness she'd also managed some underwear, a couple of tank tops, and some yoga pants. *At least I don't have to sleep naked.*

I reached for a comfortable tank that read "World's Okayest Runner" when someone knocked on my door. *Shit, now?* I dropped the towel and threw the tank over my head, before refastening the terrycloth around my waist.

"Coming."

I strode to the door and swung it open to reveal Scott on the other side holding a tray with covered dishes. We both stopped and stared at each other and I suspected my expression matched his own.

"Scott?"

"Uh, yeah." His gaze latched onto the towel riding low

on my hips. I'm sure my ribs made it look like the knot of terrycloth was too tight, but his focus remained steadfast.

"What are you doing here?" It didn't sound too hostile, I hoped.

"Uh, bringing you dinner. Dollhouse said you needed dinner." His gaze hadn't moved. "Yeah, dinner." He licked his lips and I couldn't help but laugh. That made him jerk his gaze up to my face.

"Sorry." He actually blushed and my heart melted a little.

Who knew the big, bad, cocky biker could feel chagrin?

"Where do you want me to put this?" I suspected he would've rubbed the back of his neck if he didn't need both hands to hold the tray level.

"On the table will be fine." I stepped back to let him in and he damn near skittered to the table to set down the tray. "Thanks for bringing me dinner. I thought Dollhouse would do that."

"Yeah, she got caught up in something else and said I needed to do it." Now he did rub his neck. "And I didn't mind. How you doin'? Are you okay now?"

His word choice made me bristle a little, but I tried to shove it away. *I'll never be okay.* But I would get better.

I shrugged. "I'm not sure I'll ever be okay, but I'm better than I was this afternoon."

"Do you...wanna talk about it?"

He looked so uncomfortable asking, it lightened some of my unease. "Not really. They're not memories I like to visit very often, and I already went there today."

"Yeah." Now he did rub his neck. "When you get in that head space...is there anything anyone can do for you then? Any way to make it less...I dunno, scary for you?"

Surprise shot through me. It sounded like he cared about how I felt. *Don't be ridiculous, Hunter.* He was a badass biker and I was just a pussy he wanted to tap.

I raised an eyebrow, going on the defensive. "You really want to know how to make it less scary for me?"

"Yeah. Yeah, I do. I mean, I know a little about what you're goin' through." He held up his hands when I opened my mouth to remind him he'd never know that. "I don't mean exactly or the situation that brought it about, but I meant the reactions." He shrugged. "I spent some time in the Army and I saw guys comin' back from Afghanistan and Iraq."

I raised my eyebrows. "You were in the army?"

He smirked. "What, you didn't think a badass biker could follow orders?"

"Honestly? Not at all." I shook my head.

"Tell you what, you sit down to eat and I'll tell you all about it." He waved at the table where my dinner waited.

"What about you? Don't you need dinner?" I settled into the chair and lifted the covers on the plates. "Wow."

No pizza and hot dogs for these guys. They'd brought me chicken fried steak, asparagus, and mashed potatoes with sour cream and fresh chives.

"Good, huh?" He sat across the table from me. "Grub went all the way to London for chef school, and even graduated with honors. But the stuffiness got to him and he said he needed to roam free." Scott grinned. "Not much space in England so he came home. He brought a pretty sweet 1967 Norton Commando with him, though."

I laughed, entertained by Scott's placement of value on the machinery rather than the international travel or skill set.

"I'm impressed with both the education and the motorcycle." I gestured to my plate. "And the food. Did you get anything to eat yet?"

"Yeah, I'm good. You eat what you want." He waved at me to dig in. "I just wanted to see how you were doing."

I nodded, not sure I should encourage him, but enjoying his company despite my misgivings about him at first. "So you were going to tell me all about being in the Army."

"Yeah, there isn't much to tell, really. I did a four year stint and got out. But in that time I saw a lot of the shitty results of war." He shook his head as a I dug into my meal. "I thought it would be you go over there, shoot a few people, sneak around and look cool, then come home. But it wasn't like that at all. Video games might show you what it looks like, but they don't factor in the fear, the heat or the cold, or what happens when your buddies die. I see guys gettin' frustrated when they die in the games and I'm like, dude, you just reset and you're fine. In war, there's no reset button."

I cut up my steak and asparagus into bite sized pieces as I considered his words. "Did you lose a lot of friends over there?"

He shook his head, but his shoulders tensed. "Not a lot. I didn't try to make friends. More that I was doing my time just to get through. But there were a couple of guys..." He didn't finish and I didn't press him. "When I got out, I was kinda at loose ends and Schnoz found me—Michael, I mean."

I chuckled. "Is his nickname Schnoz because of the size of his nose?"

Scott grinned. "Road name, and kinda. It's more that he can smell flowers or spices or blood from miles away. He's a huge fan of spice cake. I swear the man maps out routes based on bakers of the stuff."

I laughed. "Seriously?"

"Yup. When he's leading the ride we always stay somewhere close to a bakery."

"I'll have to remember that."

Scott paused and tipped his head. "Why, you plannin' on coming along on a ride?"

I blinked. I had been suggesting that, but it didn't make any sense. I wouldn't be here after my contracted work ended.

"No way. Motorcycles are dangerous."

"Aw, are you scared of them?"

"Yup." I didn't mind admitting it. "My cousin died in a motorcycle crash and my family made it clear the rest of us wouldn't never get near one."

"Oh, yeah, but you weren't in an accident. How do you know you won't like it?" He gave me his best smirk.

I raised an eyebrow. "How do you know I will?"

"You just need a professional to show you how it's done. Someone who knows the value of all that power between your legs."

And there's the cocky biker we were missing.

"Uh-huh." I didn't bother to respond and tucked into my meal.

"Aw, come on, Numbers. I promise to take good care of you. I wouldn't let anything happen to you."

For some reason I believed him, but I wasn't about to tell him. I needed to keep him talking about himself. "What happened when Michael found you?"

Scott shrugged. "To be honest, I don't really remember much. I was pretty much hammered off my ass. But the next day I woke up with a pounding headache, an upset stomach, and an offer to join the Concrete Angels."

"Had you ever ridden a motorcycle before?" Somehow I couldn't picture him *not* riding one.

"Yeah, but not continuously. You know, it was just a fun hobby. But Loki and Schnoz were on a recruiting mission to get some guys who had more than the usual amount of experience, and..." He paused as he tilted his head. "Flexible morals when it came to the rules set by society."

I swallowed my food. "So not straight-laced at all."

"Nope. Is that what you are?"

"I used to be before...before my assault." It was hard to admit, but it was good to say. My therapist told me the more I could talk about it the better I'd feel. Healing cost a lot, but the payment was almost always in fear.

"Yeah."

He didn't say anything for a while and I didn't feel the need to fill in the blank space. I used to be as straight-laced as they came, following the rules and the numbers, so sure I was right and doing the world good. But when my supervisor used me as his personal sex toy and no one would back me up about it, my morals became a lot more flexible to cover survival in a man's world.

"Can you tell me a way to help you out of that panicky head-space? I'm not a therapist or anything, but if I can anchor you in the here-and-now, I'll do it."

Despite my distrust of the Concrete Angels in general, I believed Scott cared and would live up to his offer. If I let him.

"So the best of the best weren't available?" I raised my eyebrows.

"How 'bout we got the best of the mediocre? Well, mediocre at therapy. I'm not anywhere close to mediocre at other things." He winked.

I laughed in spite of myself. "Okay, Scott. I need light and fresh air most of the time. But the biggest thing..."

I trailed off, afraid to admit the one thing I never received. Hell, I hadn't even told my therapist about it.

"What, Oriana?"

"I need to know someone around me I can trust to have my back and defend me against assailants when I'm most vulnerable."

That was the problem in the FBI. They all had *his* back and couldn't believe such a high ranking officer of the law would ever commit rape. He was an upstanding member of the community, a member of the PTA, a deacon of his church, and a long time FBI agent. I was considered a younger woman agent trying to make a name for myself based on ruining a highly decorated man's career.

I raised my gaze to meet Scott's beguiling green eyes. "I'm a former FBI agent in the compound of the Concrete Angels. I don't have anyone I can trust."

Scott didn't flinch or blink. "You can trust me."

CHAPTER FIVE

Scott

I'd never been so sure of anything in my life. If Oriana needed someone to trust and have her back, I'd be that guy. Part of me twinged with unease. I'd given my loyalty to Loki and the Concrete Angels, but I figured I could protect both. Numbers had signed a blood contract to work for the Club, so technically Oriana and the Concrete Angels belonged in the same class.

She must have been a mind reader because she raised an eyebrow. "I appreciate the sentiment, Scott, but I know your priority is the Concrete Angels."

She wiped her mouth and put the cover back over her empty plate. "Thanks for bringing me dinner."

Shit, how had I lost the quiet connection we'd made just a few minutes before?

"I'm definitely loyal to the Concrete Angels, but you signed a contract and work for them. That means you're an honorary Concrete Angel."

She shook her head. "It's only temporary until I solve your embezzlement problem. Then I'm a civilian once more."

If Loki allows you to leave. With the blood contract, I wasn't so sure. We'd all made blood contracts with him, though the ones the bikers made were a little different. I swallowed the thought behind my best cocky smile. "That's if you want to leave. Maybe you'll decide to stay."

"So far I haven't found much reason to do so."

"I'm hoping to change your mind." I held out my hands for the tray. "How 'bout I take this back to the clubhouse for you while you get started on those files. What do you like to drink? Do you need anything to keep the brain firing while workin'?"

Oriana raised her eyebrows. "How do you know about that?"

I shrugged. "I noticed it with Neo, and Dollhouse when she's workin' on some architectural plans. She has to have lemonade next to her so she can keep her focus and creativity up."

"Dollhouse is an architect?"

"Yeah, didn't she tell you that? She has a degree from Montana State University's architectural school. It's one of the best in the country."

"Whoa, really?" Oriana looked impressed.

"Yeah." I smirked. "What, did you think all the women did here was look pretty and fuck?"

A blush suffused her face as she looked away and shrugged. "I guess I did since she told me Loki found her at a brothel. I didn't realize she had such a strong education."

"Pretty much all the Angels have kick-ass backgrounds." I narrowed my eyes and waggled a finger. "Don't judge a book by its cover, Numbers. Dollhouse got her road name from building to-scale models of most of the CA's holdings. Hell, she even designed this place when we took it over for renovations." I headed for the door. "So what are you drinkin'?"

"Uh, I don't know. Ice water, I guess."

"Ice water comin' up. I'll be back."

I sauntered out the door and into the yard just as Roy revved up his bike and gestured to Mel to get on. She shot a look toward her former cabin, her expression a mixture of sadness and frustration before she dropped her gaze and wrapped her hair in a ponytail. I didn't have much sympathy for her. She'd lied to Oriana to get her up here and I didn't think Oriana would forgive easily. Yeah, I lied when I had to and Mel's lies helped me immensely, but something told me I'd have to be fuckin' honest if I wanted a chance with Oriana.

Roy met my gaze and nodded before he gunned the bike and shot for the gate. Mel squealed and grabbed his waist to keep from falling off the back. *That guy's an asshole.* I'd never win any etiquette or decorum pageants, but Roy made me look like a fuckin' gentleman. I never really liked the guy. He put me on edge, made me choose my words carefully when around him.

Shaking my head, I continued into the clubhouse and almost ran into Samurai standing just inside the doors.

"Oh, hey man, sorry about that."

He neatly side-stepped me and nodded. "It's no problem. Do you know where Roy is going?"

"Yeah, he said he had to run into Denver to check on some contacts. Why?"

Samurai grunted as he watched Roy clear the gate. "Didn't clear it with Loki."

Oh, shit. As members of the Concrete Angels, Loki gave us a lot of latitude when it came to making shit happen. He wasn't into micro-managing. But we had to keep him up to date with our dealings and when we met with contacts. We didn't need to brief him in detail, but a message, text, email, or mention was required. That Roy hadn't done so made me frown.

"He say anything to you about it?" Sam fixed me with his intense stare.

"Nope. He just said he was gonna take Mel with him to cheer her up while he did his business."

Sam grunted again. "Guess I'm gonna follow him then. Loki said something felt off."

I narrowed my eyes. "This a search-and-destroy thing?"

Sam shook his head. "Just recon."

I nodded. "'Kay. Keep me in the loop when you find anything out."

Sam raised his eyebrows. "Why?"

"Dunno. Gut feeling." Something about Roy was bugging me, but I couldn't point to a single thing that made me uneasy.

He dipped his chin once. "Got it. Will do." He slipped past me through the door and headed for his bike. He didn't ride a Harley, but his Yamaha Ninja had earned its stripes. He'd been part of a Yakuza biker gang and no one in the Concrete Angels gave him shit for it.

I carried the tray back to the kitchen where Grub sat back sipping whiskey and watching his crew clean up. I nodded to him as I set the tray down next to the dirty dishes and he nodded back.

"Dollhouse was looking for ya."

"Thanks, Grub. I'll track her down."

"You do that. Hey, did the Fed lady like the food?" Despite his relaxed posture, his shoulders tensed.

"Yeah, she did. She was real impressed."

His shoulders relaxed. "Good, good. Wanna make sure she eats well."

My shoulders tensed. "Oh yeah? Why?"

Grub shook his head and frowned. "I dunno. She needs it, somehow. She doesn't look like she's been eatin' well. And good food is the basis for a good life."

I let out the breath I hadn't known I'd held. "Can't argue with you there, Grub."

I waved as I stepped back out into the main room and

headed for the bar, trying to shove my tension away. I'd been worried Grub had a personal interest in Oriana and jealousy had never been my thing. *So why the fuck is it coming up now?*

I didn't have an answer as I stopped at the bar beside Dollhouse and asked Karma for an ice water.

"How's Numbers doing?" Karma asked the question, but Dollhouse turned her head to look at me with the same question in her eyes.

"She's...better I think. She ate everything and wants some ice water." I nodded to Karma as she set down the glass in front of me.

"Is she gonna be okay? It scared the daylights outta me when she collapsed." Dollhouse rubbed her face with her hands.

"Yeah, I think she'll be fine." I hoped so, and I hoped she'd believed me when I told her I'd have her back. "She's had a fuckin' crazy-ass day comin' here. She'll be better tomorrow."

"And what about you? Are you gonna be okay now?" Dollhouse raised an eyebrow.

I barked a short laugh. "What the hell's that supposed to mean?"

She shrugged. "I heard Schnoz damn near put you through a tree because you were bein' a twitchy jackass."

I ground my teeth to keep from telling her to fuck off. She was right, but I hated everyone knowing about my jealous outburst with Michael.

"Yeah, I'm done bein' a twitchy jackass and I'm just bringing her some water."

"Good." Dollhouse nodded sharply. "I'm glad it worked."

"Glad what worked?" I grasped the sweating glass, not sure I wanted to hear the answer.

"You bringin' her dinner." She shot me a smug smile. "If she wants you to bring her ice water, she likes you enough to let you back in. My plan worked."

"What plan is that?"

"Getting you together with Numbers. Duh."

I rolled my eyes. "I'm pretty sure I could get together with her on my own. I don't need your help."

"Oh yeah? She wouldn't have let you back in there without the tray full of food." She stood up and pantomimed a basketball free throw. "She shoots, she scores. And the crowd goes wild."

Both she and Karma hissed like the muted roar of a sports crowd with their hands in the air. I shook my head and took the ice water off the bar, heading for the door. As annoying as my little sister could be, she was also a born romantic and would do anything to see her friends and family happy. Not that I believed in romance. I believed in sex and attraction and good times. But romance?

Romance required commitment and effort and putting someone else first. Hell, I didn't think I had a romantic bone in my body, certainly not a non-selfish one. But as I headed out the door to bring Numbers her water, I had the sneaking suspicion I was lying to myself.

CHAPTER SIX

Oriana

What the hell have I gotten myself into?
I'd already asked myself that question at least a hundred times just for being in the compound held by the Concrete Angels, but now it had become about the mess of funds transfers and money manipulation within their accounts.

The mishmash of accounts the motorcycle club held was an accounting nightmare.

"How the hell do they keep track of their cash?" I shook my head as I stared at the computer.

I'd been going over Loki's records for the last two days and near as I could tell the Concrete Angels had their fingers in pretty much every pie conceivable. I'd found accounts for high end vehicle sales, designer drugs for the trust-fund rich kids, even shipments of expensive accessories like handbags, sunglasses, wrist watches, and shoes. They had accounts for selling mainstream drugs and alcohol, but also weaponry, both new and outdated, across state lines and international borders. *The ATF would have a field day with these* guys.

The only things they didn't seem to be into were human trafficking and contract killing. *Thank goodness.* I might be former FBI, but selling people was a line I couldn't cross, and assassins made me shoot first and ask questions later.

But following the money trails for all these enterprises was like investigating a giant anthill stirred up by an angry toddler. Some intersected and some never touched. Some of the businesses were legitimate, paying taxes and licensing fees on time. Others were more shady, running so far under the table as to be considered part of the rug.

Loki's organization of all these different accounts made no sense to me. I had no idea how he'd figured out someone was embezzling from him, but he swore money had gone missing. After two days of reorganizing things into a pattern I could understand, I'd finally had a basic understanding of what his business looked like. And holy shit, the man was an entraprenurial genius.

He made money hand over fist in multiple markets, laundering the money from the shady shit through his legitimate businesses. But instead of spending the proceeds on flashy crap, he dumped most of his money back into the businesses at a different point, constantly renewing itself and keeping the whole system flush. I was impressed with his brilliance and ingenuity.

But he'd been so disorganized, I had a tough time figuring out where he was losing money.

Unless the accounts were such a mess that he only thought he was losing money.

I frowned as I finished the updated spreadsheet list of all the revenue streams for the Concrete Angels. Overall, they appeared flush with cash and money easily moved from one place to another. I sighed and rubbed my eyes, sitting back in my chair. There didn't appear to be anything wrong at first glance.

I snorted. *At the thousandth glance, either.* There was no way anyone would be able to tell someone embezzled money from the disorganized mess.

I sat up and pulled my hands from my eyes. *Maybe that was the point.* Maybe the disorganization had given the perpetrator the opportunity, if not the motive. The embezzler could have done it by accident the first few times, but when it went unnoticed, it became an easy way to skim off the top and into his or her own pockets.

That meant the perpetrator probably didn't want me here finding their enterprise and might try to cover their tracks. Hell, they may have already started the process when Loki announced I'd been brought in just for the purpose of plugging the leak.

I reached for my bottle of water and found it empty. Blinking in surprise, I shot a look out my cabin's windows to find dusk had painted the sky with the rosy tones of sunset.

"Shit, what time is it?"

I'd picked up the habit of talking to myself after I left the FBI just to hear another human voice once in a while. My therapist had said it came from isolating myself, but it wasn't a bad thing. She just wanted to make sure I got out and interacted from time to time.

"I should really get some dinner."

I saved my work on the computer and logged out of the network before locking down my terminal. While all the information belonged to the Concrete Angels, I didn't want just anyone to wander in and take a look at all my hard work in organization. I figured Neo could come in and break into the laptop without much effort - hell, he even knew my password to the network - but the rest of the crew didn't have that kind of skill. *I hope.*

I rose from my chair and headed to the kitchenette to wash my hands, shaking my head. How would I know what kinds of skills the different members of the Concrete

Angels had? They continually surprised me. Dollhouse was a professional architect. A woman named Calhoun had a degree in Physics and Engineering. Turned out Scott was a master negotiator despite his brash personality. He could get just about anything out of anyone when he set his mind to it. The men and women of the Concrete Angels came from all walks of life and all educational backgrounds. But one thing they all had in common: shrewd intelligence.

It's a damn good thing I'm currently on their side.

I dried my hands as my stomach growled. I couldn't remember the last time I'd eaten anything and no one had brought me a meal since the morning.

I'm gonna have to face them at some point.

I swallowed hard and checked the clock. Seven forty-two. It was later than I'd thought and dinner might be completely over. My stomach growled again and I grimaced. I needed to eat something. Maybe the lateness of the hour would mean there'd be fewer people around. Fewer people to stare at me with pity or hostililty.

I closed my eyes. I remembered those looks from the last few weeks at the FBI and my stomach cramped from fear rather than hunger. It still hurt. The looks told me it was my fault. My fault I'd been raped. My fault I lost my job.

I couldn't face those looks again.

I braced my hands on my kitchen counter and forced myself to take deep breaths. Fear would only keep me a prisoner. What were a few looks, really? It said more about them than it did about me. I knew the truth of my past. I'd lived it, been there for it. They knew nothing and their opinions about it meant nothing to me. These weren't my people or my family. None of them had my back.

Scott has your back. Michael does, too.

The thought came out of nowhere, like a blazing shaft of light through the clouds after a thunderstorm. Scott promised and Michael wouldn't deliberately hurt me.

Unless I screwed over the Concrete Angels, they'd have my back as much as their biker siblings. For the first time in over two years, I wasn't technically alone.

I took a shuddering breath and stood up, opening my eyes. Maybe I could do this. Maybe I could face the rest of the club in the dining room. Maybe their opinions didn't really affect me because I wasn't trying to impress them. I just had to impress Loki, and I was well on my way to doing that with the work I'd done in the last two days.

He doesn't know that, Hunter.

No, but he would tomorrow. Now that I had the accounts organized, it'd be much easier to see the patterns of embezzlement.

A tentative smile curved my lips as I headed into my bedroom to check my appearance. I had to make sure I was dressed to be in public. I'd often forgotten to get dressed or shower when I isolated myself and I didn't want to do that here.

I found I'd at least put on a T-shirt and shorts, but they appeared as if I'd lived in them for days. So did my body. My hair looked like I'd spent a lot of time pulling it into some retro '80s style with too much hairspray. *Dude, did you totally see Loki's accounts though? Like gag me with a pitchfork.* The Valley Girl accent in my head made me laugh as I took myself into the shower to wash her away.

I forced myself to focus on the present moment as my therapist taught me so I didn't get too worked up about facing the rest of the club members. Mel had thoughtfully packed me a cute V-necked tank top and a pair of bejeweled capris that hadn't seen the light of day for over three years. Stress had allowed me to release some weight. *Just ignore the ribs sticking out.*

I finished my shower and dressed in the tank top and capris then brushed out my hair and grabbed my keys as I stepped out the door. But I hesitated on the threshold and eyed the laptop on the table. I'd logged out so no one could get in without Neo's help, but that wouldn't stop someone from snagging it and cracking it elsewhere. I darted back inside and took the laptop into my bedroom, shoving it between the mattress and the box springs.

Better. I locked up the cabin and headed for the clubhouse.

A few of the Scooters were still in the yard, but not the guy who'd accosted me a few days earlier. I'm sure he was around somewhere, but I'd just as soon not see him again. My summer outfit wasn't much of a deterrent to a determined asshole.

Instead, I straightened my shoulders and strode to the clubhouse like there was somewhere I needed to be. I didn't look around, but kept an eye on them peripherally. None of them made a move toward me as I shoved through the clubhouse doors.

Though there were several people hanging around watching TV or playing pool, the club's hierarchy was conspicuously absent. I shot a look at the offices around the main room, but all the doors remained closed. Country music played in the background and a few people danced. Most of the men had a honey hanging on him, some male and some female. *Hey, whichever floats your boat.* A few of the female honeys watched me walk to the dining area with narrowed eyes as if trying to determine my role as competition.

I mentally shook my head. I hadn't come for the sex.

Fortunately, the buffet remained in place and I served myself some real fried chicken, mashed potatoes, fried zucchini cubes, and a roll with bits of rosemary in it. My mouth watered and my stomach rumbled as I carried my plate to a table and settled in. The first bite of food damn near made me swoon and I moaned with pleasure.

"Damn, Grub must've outdone himself tonight if you moan like that." Karma's voice intruded in my savory experience. I opened my eyes to find her grinning at me.

"I don't know what he normally cooks like, but this is damn good food." I took the time to drink some water before getting back to my meal.

"Are you feeling better? We haven't seen much of you in the last couple of days." Karma settled into the chair across from me.

I shrugged and nodded. "Just going through the financial records. They're all over the place. It's taken me a while to untangle them."

Understatement of the year. Cooked spaghetti was less snarled.

"That bad, huh?"

I nodded again. "I can understand why embezzlement happened. If no one's clear on where the money is coming from or how much, it's easy to skim off the top. I don't know how Loki noticed."

"Have you found who did it?" A curious tightness filled Karma's voice.

I pretended not to notice, but I filed that away for consideration. "Not yet. I just got the records straightened out. I'll start looking for patterns tomorrow."

"Perfect." Her tone changed to forced brightness as she smiled. "You should take tonight off and relax a little. Play some pool."

I shook my head. "Nah. I'm not good company as an outsider. I'm just going to eat and head back to my cabin. Loki's not paying me to hang out."

"Aw, come on. Loki and his guys can afford to give you some break time. Hell, if it was up to them, no one would work." She grinned. "Loosen up, Numbers. You would love pool. It's all about the numbers."

"It's about the angles, which is geometry, not numbers. I didn't say I hadn't played, I said I should get back to work." I kept eating. "The sooner I figure out your embezzler, the sooner you can be rid of me."

She raised her eyebrows. "You think we want to get rid

of you?"

I snorted. "Come on, Karma. I'm a former FBI agent in a notorious motorcycle club. I bet you can't see my taillights fast enough."

Karma tilted her head, her expression turning serious. "That's not it at all, actually. A lot of us are glad you're here. If we're losing money, that's bad for the club."

"I'm not buying it." I shook my head as I finished my meal. "Y'all are tolerating me. I'll never be one of the in-crowd here, and y'all will be worried about what I know. Hell, I'd bet dollars to doughnuts you won't actually let me leave when I'm done."

Her expression shifted to curiously blank and she wouldn't meet my eyes.

Oh shit, they're not going to let me leave.

Panic shot through my system and I gripped the arms of my chair to keep from bolting. Could I get out of this somehow? I'd seen their records, yes, but only to organize them into coherency. I hadn't found the embezzler and I hadn't really figured out which money came from what enterprise. I could conceivably walk away without exposing them.

Yeah, like they'd believe that. I'd seen the records, that was enough. They wouldn't believe I was unaware of the financial sources. I had to figure out a way to get free of the Concrete Angels, but at the moment my mind sat blank. There was a reason why nefarious groups found a moneyman and keep him or her indefinitely. They couldn't afford to dismiss someone who knew all their secrets.

"Oh sweet glory." I swallowed hard to keep my dinner down. "I'm gonna be stuck here with people who hate me because I know too much. Or worse, I'll have an 'accident' and my body will never be found."

Karma barked a laugh, though she still wouldn't meet my eyes. "You gotta stop believing what you see on TV about motorcycle clubs."

I tilted my head and shot her a dry look. "I'm former FBI. I didn't learn this on TV."

"Yeah, well, even the FBI doesn't know everything about us, despite what they think they know." Karma sat back and crossed her arms over her chest. "We have legit businesses and pay taxes. Hell, we even give to charities."

"I know. I've seen the records."

"So, what's the big deal?"

"Do I really need to explain the problem of a former FBI agent hanging with a more than "legit" motorcycle club?" I snorted as I shook my head. It was time to change the subject. "Where is everyone anyway? I expected them to be in here hanging out."

She shrugged. "They had some business to check out in Denver this afternoon. They should be back in a few. You done eating?"

"Yeah, why?"

"We're gonna play a game of pool so you can relax a little." She helped gather some of dinner items to take to the cleaning bins.

"But—"

"Come on, I know you're waitin' on Scott. This will distract you and pass the time." She dumped my dishes in the bins. "You need something other than work, Numbers."

"I'm not—"

Karma didn't wait as she headed for the pool tables in the back of the room. *Dammit, I'm not waiting for Scott.* But she'd already waved away some of the guys standing around the green felted table and racked the balls. I'd look like an ornery bitch if I didn't at least join her.

"Come on, Numbers. I promise you'll like it." She waved me over.

Oh, I knew I'd like it. I hadn't played in a while, but that didn't mean I didn't know how. In fact, most of the forensic accounting section in the Denver office of the FBI wouldn't play with me because they couldn't beat me. I was too good. I'd actually joined a couple of competitions and made big bucks while studying for my degrees in college.

I shuffled toward the table, biting my lower lip. I didn't want to piss Karma off. She was one of the few Concrete Angels who seemed to like me. At least she was nice to me. I'd have to miss a few shots to make it a bit more fair. Hell, that might even make it a challenge. Could I play "badly" enough to make me average?

"All right. Maybe a few games."

Karma grinned. "Grab a cue and let's do this."

I selected one of the cues from the inset cabinet on the wall and tested its weight and balance before I turned back to the table. The men who'd been lounging around shifted out of the way, probably to get a better view of our asses when we bent over, and settled in chairs around the room.

"No tits on the table!" The shout came from behind Karma and she flipped her middle finger up without looking.

"You break, Numbers."

I lined up the cue ball and sighted down my arm. It wasn't unlike sighting down the barrel of a weapon, but this was far more fun. I took my perfect position to sink as many balls as possible and shifted just a little to the left. No point in dissuading Karma to play with me right from the get-go.

I sent the cue ball into the colorful triangle and the balls exploded apart with a satisfying clack. A few dropped in the pockets and started the game on stripes. Despite trying to make it a challenge, most of the shots were easy for me, so I purposefully messed up the third one so Karma could have a shot.

I stood back and watched her line up to shoot, silently critiquing her form. I'd learned a long time ago to keep my thoughts to myself, but I evaluated my opponent and figured out the weaknesses in her game. I shoved my competitive side into the corner and tried to just play for fun.

Karma wasn't too bad a player and she held her own pretty well, but I made sure to flub shots and throw a couple of games to appear as a skilled but average player. My days of ruling the pool tables were behind me. Despite my best efforts, though, a crowd of Concrete Angels and their honeys, the women they got to enjoy who weren't attached to any one member, gathered to watch us play. They whistled and cheered when some spectacular shot was made.

"Damn, Numbers can shoot."

"Fuck yeah. I got a ten spot that says she wins the next game."

And just like that, the betting started.

CHAPTER SEVEN

Scott

Shit, I was bone-tired and hungry and hot, and not in a good way. Samurai had followed Roy into Denver but lost him in some of the seedier parts of town. Neo had tracked him using his cell phone, but Roy turned it off and we were left searching the old-fashioned way. That meant a few of us had to head into town to chase him down.

My gut still grumbled about Roy and his motives. Something about this latest trip of his was hinky but I couldn't put my finger on what. Fortunately, Loki and Schnoz felt something too.

Two days of fruitless searching turned up nothing but rumor until Roy turned his phone back on when he hit the Longmont exit. We scrambled, headed home before it looked suspicious to him. *Not that we're the ones doing something suspicious.* Melrose's phone had been on, but she'd spent the entire two days at a downtown hotel ordering Netflix and room service. Apparently, her attitude hadn't improved enough for Roy to get laid. He never visited her there.

Frustration made me snarl as I shoved my way into the clubhouse. But I came to an abrupt stop as a damn fine ass in bejeweled denim met my gaze.

"Holy fuck, Scott. Your woman sure does know how to shoot." Indiana, a guy who was the spitting image of the original Han Solo, slapped me on the shoulder, his appreciative gaze glued to Oriana's backside.

She's not mine. Yet. I wanted her to be, but I hadn't figured out how to make the move and claim her. She'd made it pretty clear she didn't like the club's way of doing things and she wouldn't be my anything. But I wasn't giving up anytime soon.

"Yeah, well, keep your eyes off her ass while you're watchin' her." I shoved him out of the way and headed closer to the pool tables.

Oriana sank her shot and stood up, grinning as the crowd erupted into appreciative whistles.

"Damn, honey, that was sweeter than a blowjob." Karma shook her head with admiration.

"Are you talking about the drink or the activity?" Oriana smirked as she lined up her next shot. "Twelve in the side."

"The activity. Which side? That one?" Karma pointed to the pocket to Oriana's left. "You're gonna make that in there? This I gotta see."

"Watch and learn."

Oriana bent over the table, her expression settling into intense focus. She sighted, drew a deep breath then released it a bit and snapped her wrist. The cue hit the cue ball and the damn thing danced around the table, careening off the bumpers, and brushing the six ball to knock the twelve into the side just as she predicted. It also left the cue ball lined up with the eight to make an easy shot into the corner pocket.

The crowd exploded into cheers as she sauntered around the table, winked at Karma, and sank the eight without scratching. She stood up and leaned on her cue.

"You really think my pool shots are sweeter than a blowjob?" She shook her head. "You must not be doing it right."

The crowd erupted into shouts of amusement and surprise along with whistles of appreciation. It made me laugh and my dick get hard. *Damn, how would she know the art of a good blowjob?* I didn't know but I wanted to find out.

Karma laughed and nodded. "Yeah, probably not since I prefer a guy to go down on me."

"Oh glory, I won't say no to that. Should I rack the balls for another game?" Oriana twirled the triangle rack between her fingers.

"Yeah, rack 'em hard, Numbers!" Someone shouted it from the back of the room.

"Bring 'em close enough and I'll grant your wish." She swung the cue like a baseball bat.

"How would you know what a good blowjob is, Numbers?" I stepped into the circle of people surrounding the table, my anger and frustration draining away.

She rolled her eyes as she gathered the balls out of the pockets. "Wouldn't you like to know?"

"Hell yeah." I sauntered over to stand behind her. "If you think you know so much, why don't I take you back to my cabin for a little pocket pool?" I waggled my eyebrows and the guys around us whistled again. But she shook her head.

"Sorry, I only play on the table."

"Fine with me." I strode to the cue rack and selected one. "Let's play a game and winner gets their choice."

Oriana raised a brow as she shifted her weight to one leg. "What do I get if I win?"

I shrugged. "Whatever you want, sweetheart."

"The first thing will be you don't get to call me pet names." She narrowed her eyes. "What do you get if you

85

win?"

"Whatever I want, but we can start with your best blowjob."

A smirk creased her lips and I had a momentary pang of unease as she nodded. "Okay."

"Hold up." Loki's voice filled the gap as Oriana racked the balls. "I think this needs to be a bit more interesting."

I swallowed hard. It was never good when Loki wanted things more interesting. "Oh yeah? What did you have in mind?"

"Let's make this strip pool. For each game you lose, you take off an item of clothing, *ja*?" He waved at them both. "You look like you each have enough to go for a few games at least. Whoever's left with the most clothing at the end of, say, five games wins."

I grinned. "Sounds good to me. You game, Numbers?"

"Yup. You break." She smirked and some of my bravado left. I was a damn good pool player, but if she was this confident, I'd have to watch out.

Shit-oh-dear, I had no idea.

I sank a couple of balls on the break and went for solids. But after missing the second shot. I didn't get another chance to touch the cue ball until after she sank all her balls and the eight without scratching. By the fifth game, I was down to my shirt and jeans, and Loki held up his hands to quiet the laughter and betting.

"I think it's been unfair, *ja*? You didn't tell us you were a pool shark, Ms. Hunter."

"You didn't ask." She tilted her head with a smirk. "I believe that by your own rules, I've won, and I get my choice of what we do."

Loki nodded with his own smirk. "*Ja*, that's true. But I'm gonna change the rules. Because I can."

She narrowed her eyes. "Of course, you are. I wouldn't expect anything less."

He shrugged. "It's my nature. So, now, since you've

won five games, Ms. Hunter, you must remove a sandal
now and lose another item for every three games you win,
until one of you is naked."

"Aw, come on. That's not fair." I scowled at Loki.
"She's already kicked my ass."

"Who said anything about 'fair'?" He widened his eyes
in mock-incredulity.

"But I'm already down to just my jeans and shirt."

"Then you best play better, *ja*?" He waved at the table.
"Your break, Scott."

I swallowed hard and lined up for the break. I didn't
really want to have my dick hanging out while Oriana
whupped my ass at pool, but at the moment I didn't have a
choice. I hadn't bothered to put on any underwear this
morning so now my ass would be on display. Literally.

My break wasn't bad at all. I managed to sink three of
the solids and two stripes. *Solids it is.* I scanned the table to
find the best shot that would leave me with a continuing
shot. The seven and the three were both promising, but the
seven would leave me with more options. I made my shot
and satisfaction surged as the ball sank and gave me at least
three additional shots.

I sank the next one, but flubbed the third, and shot a
look at Oriana as the crowd murmured their thoughts on my
performance. Gone was the guarded, quiet woman who
worked with numbers. In her place stood an intense
predator waiting for her chance to pounce. Arousal shot
through me and my dick pressed against the zipper of my
jeans. This was the sexiest I'd ever seen her and my heart
thundered with the idea of her chasing me.

What can I say? I love a woman with confidence.

Despite my imminent nudity, I loved watching her take
control of the table. She moved with grace and precision,
and I'd never been so happy to lose my shirt in my life. She
ruled the table and took it in a clean sweep, sinking all of
her balls and the eight with grace. She licked her lips as I

tossed my shirt on top of my cut.

"Nice sleeve." She nodded to my right arm covered in ink from shoulder to knuckles. "It suits you."

"You like ink, Numbers?" Indiana called from the back. "I'll show you some damn fine ink when you kick Scott's ass."

Oriana rolled her eyes as she racked the balls again. "Break 'em, Scott."

Something about the way she gestured to the table gave me the impression that it was just her and I in her world. She managed to push away the audience and focus on me and the game. I tried to do the same as I sent the cue ball into the tight triangle of colored balls. This time I sank more stripes than solids, and I knew I'd have to play well enough to keep the cue ball in my possession, or I was done.

I kept my focus despite my bare feet on the floor and the audience staring at the huge tat on my back. The ink was there to cover a large burn scar I'd gotten when my paternal uncle went on a drunken rampage and threw a pot of scalding water at me. He was currently serving back to back life sentences in Leavenworth for the damage he caused his family and others while in drunken rages. I didn't miss him.

I lined up my shots and kept my attention from wandering to Oriana's avid focus on the table. I sank all the balls but one and missed the mark on the last one. *Aw shit. She's gonna take me for a ride now.* And not the kind of ride I'd been hoping for. The crowd groaned for me and I grimaced before stepping back.

"All yours, sweetheart."

"Damn straight, and you'll stop calling me pet names." She raised her chin before she settled in to finish the game.

But the damnedest thing happened. She actually scratched on the eight. We all stood there dumbfounded in disbelief for about ten seconds before the room exploded in cheers and surprise. I met Oriana's gaze and she smiled ruefully as she pulled off her other sandal and tossed it with the first one.

"Rack 'em, big boy. Let's see if I can put you to bed."

I laughed, more than happy to be put to bed with her. At this point, even if I lost, I won. I had a feeling Oriana wanted some alone time with me as much as I wanted it with her. I'd missed her while we'd been in Denver ferreting out what the hell Roy was doing. I'd never missed one of the honeys before. They were always there to scratch an itch, but I didn't get attached. Oriana hadn't done anything remotely sexual with me and I missed hearing her voice and verbally sparring with her.

I shook my head as I collected the balls and threw them into the rack, tightening them in to a solid triangle. *It doesn't make sense.* I'd known her less than a week and I was already thinking about her all the time. I lifted the rack away and stood back, puzzling over the odd sense that I'd met someone important.

Oriana broke the balls apart into a perfect arrangement and I didn't touch the cue ball once in the game. Usually when I lost I was pretty frustrated, but I'd been beaten a few games ago and I just laughed when she sank the eight. *Aw hell, I knew I was done for a while ago.* I set the cue up in its rack and reached for the button on my jeans while the guys around me hooted and hollered.

"Wait." Oriana's voice cracked like a whip and the whole place shut up. "Since Scott's my prize, and I don't share prizes, I think I'll have him do the final reveal in private."

She grinned as the hooting became encouraging and a few guys shouted for me to take it all off. I matched her grin with a wink but left the fly closed so the jeans wouldn't slide off my hips.

"Whatever you want, sweetheart."

"Strike one, Scott." She tsked and shook her finger at

me. "No pet names."

"What about road names?" If she didn't want road names, I'd have to tell her my given name and I'd left that one behind so long ago now it no longer fit me.

"Those are fine." She deposited her cue and turned to me. "Gather your things and lead the way."

I bent over and grabbed my clothes and boots. "Where are we goin'?"

"Your place." She shoved her feet into her sandals. "I want to see how the badass biker lives in his natural habitat."

I laughed as I headed for the door of the clubhouse, a cocksure smile creasing my lips. The other guys thought I'd lost, but the way I figured it, I'd won. Schnoz had told me I had to wait for Oriana to come to me, and my barely held patience had succeeded. I didn't know what she had in mind to do with me, but there was a good chance I could give her the pleasure she needed. I hoped she needed it. I didnt know how women thought, but I didn't think they were too different from men when it came to sex. Yeah, I know what society says, but I think that's a load of horseshit, personally.

Oriana followed me amid cheers and hoots of lascivious nature, but I didn't care. She was comin' with me and that was damn near perfect. The gravel of the yard outside dug into the soles of my feet as I strode for my cabin beside Oriana's. The sky had darkened as a late thunderstorm rolled in over the Rockies. The clouds flickered with lightning zigzagging through them but no rain fell yet.

"Looks like it'll be a helluva storm." Oriana's voice floated to my ears and I realized she'd stopped.

I turned and caught her staring up at the sky, watching the lightning creating electric lace through the clouds. The wind kicked up and blew her hair away from her face. She looked relaxed and content for the first time since she'd come to the Concrete Angels' compound.

It was the most fucking beautiful thing I'd seen in a long time. I held my breath, wanting to preserve the moment for as long as I could. *What the hell can I do to make her that content here in the future?* I'd just have to start with tonight and hope she got addicted to the pleasure I could give her.

"Yeah, I'd like to get inside since I'm standing out here in bare feet and no shirt."

She dropped her gaze to my body and my nipples hardened as she examined my chest.

"We can't have that." She gestured toward my cabin with one hand. "We'd best get you inside then."

I didn't have to be told twice. I hurried to my door just as the rain came sheeting down and we skittered inside before the wall of water blotted out the yard. She squealed as she slid ast me and we both laughed behind the closed door.

"That was close." Her eyes sparkled and my cock hardened in my undone jeans. "How 'bout you show me my prize now?"

I grinned. "Yes, ma'am." I pushed down the zipper and slid the jeans off my hips.

She gasped and bit her bottom lip, her eyes lighting up as my cock stiffened in front of her. I was decent sized. I'd never been considered small, but her delight did wonders for my ego.

"Damn, I knew you were good looking when I saw you walk up to the car, but sweet glory..." She raised her gaze to mine. "You're beautiful, Scott." Then she blushed as if she'd said something wrong.

The word didn't show up much in the compliments I'd received, but I'd take it from her. Her assertion of my beauty meant more than any compliment from the honeys who hung around the compound. *What the hell is wrong with me?* Except it didn't feel wrong. The idea that she found me beautiful made my chest swell with pride and I damn near strutted in front of her. I *wanted* to be beautiful for her.

"Hey, that's a damn fine compliment coming from you, swe– er, Numbers. I like knowing you like what you see." I held my arms out to the sides so nothing was covered.

"Oh, I do. I also like that you go commando. That's sexy as hell." She licked her lips. "Turn around for me so I can see all of you."

My cock jerked with arousal and precum dripped from the tip as I kicked the jeans from my ankles to turn in a circle. She hummed her approval until I faced her again and she nodded with satisfaction suffusing her features.

"You're what wet dreams are made of." She sighed as she waved toward my bedroom. "Let's go into your room so I can fully enjoy my prize."

Hell yeah. I sauntered into the bedroom, enjoying the feeling of her eyes on my back and ass. Yeah, my uncle had burned me, but the ink obscured the scar and I'd worked hard to make the muscles look good. I wouldn't describe myself as a gym rat, but I kept myself fit for occasions like this.

I turned on the light beside the bed before I set up the pillows so I could lean against them. I pulled back the Transformers comforter to expose the clean sheets and settled into them on my back. My cock lay against my belly, straining in a hard curve as she stopped at the foot of the bed.

"Are you gonna get undressed?" I threw my hands behind my head, trying to relax even as my heart pounded with excitement.

She tilted her head with a smirk. "I just wanted to look at you for a moment. It's not often I get a man to lay there quietly. Besides, I try to enjoy beauty when I find it and…" She gave a soft whistle in appreciation. "You definitely qualify as beautiful."

"Yeah, but I'm like a hands-on exhibit. You can't get the full effect unless you touch me." I winked and she laughed.

"I like completely interactive." She took off her sandals and crawled onto the bed, still fully clothed. "Let's see if I can get the reaction I want."

She settled on her belly between my legs, trailing the fingers of one hand up from my knee to my crotch. Electric fire skittered in the wake of her sensual caress and I moaned. She smiled enough to make my cock jerk in front of her and her focus shifted to my groin.

"You smell good."

She nuzzled my balls and I tightened my hands in the sheets to keep from grabbing her head. Fuck, it was hard to wait for the pleasure I knew was coming, but I didn't want to screw it up. *Schnoz said I had to wait.* I gritted my teeth as she slid her hands over my hips and up my sides as she used her nose to tickle my balls.

Wait, that's not her nose.

Wet heat slid over my scrotum, igniting pleasure more powerful than I'd felt in a long time. None of the honeys did this to me. They weren't about finesse or foreplay. They just grabbed my dick and sucked hard. Oriana tantalized and teased and took her time. It was both excruciating and magnificent all at the same time.

"Oh, glory, Oriana. That feels fuckin' awesome."

"I aim to please."

The purr in her voice made my cock jerk and I moaned. How the hell could a woman sound so sexy while licking my balls? But then she grasped my shaft and licked all the way up to the head. I lost coherency when she fitted her mouth around my stiff flesh.

Damn, it's like sitting in a hot tub. That's what it felt like to have my cock in Oriana's talented mouth. Wet heat, pressure, and the gentle rub of her tongue on my dick made my eyes roll back in my head.

Sweet glory, never let this end.

A line from an old cowboy movie skittered across my awareness. Oriana could suck the chrome off a trailer hitch, but she also had the exquisite ability to polish it back to a high shine. Sweet glory, the woman had a clever and talented tongue, and each stroke over my flesh set me ablaze.

I tried to hold back as my orgasm reached screaming levels. I let go of the sheets and grasped her head with one hand as she bobbed up and down on my shaft. I wasn't sure if I tried to hold her there or pull her off, but she hummed with what sounded like approval.

"Holy shit, I'm gonna come, Oriana."

She pulled off long enough to say, "That's the point." She returned to her task and I lost track of time.

Hot, erotic pleasure boiled up from my balls and flooded through my body until I was lost in the wash. Hot jets of cum shot from my cock down her throat, but she swallowed it all, humming with delight. I let myself go, enjoying her efforts and one thought came through clearly.

Holy fuck, I think I love this woman.

CHAPTER EIGHT

Oriana

A huge sense of accomplishment washed over me as Scott groaned and arched his back, shoving his cock deep into my mouth. I swallowed down his cum as his cock grew thicker in my mouth. I loved his taste and his scent – warm, rich, masculine, and sexy as hell. I was pretty sure just about all the other women in the compound had sampled his 'wares', but to have the courage to do this, right now, seemed a huge accomplishment.

I could feel arousal. I could take pleasure in giving it to someone else. Those were mile markers I never thought I'd reach. And I hit them with the cockiest biker I'd ever met, a man I'd never have trusted to get me there in a million years.

"Holy fuck, Oriana. You're a goddess at giving head." He panted as he lay against the pillows of his bed.

"I'm going to take that as a compliment." I sat back and pulled my tank over my head and tossed it to the floor.

"Holy shit, you weren't wearing a bra the whole time?" His jaw dropped and his eyes glazed over.

"That's why I had to win. I can't just whip my shirt off in front of everyone like you."

"Don't let that stop you on my account." He sat up and reached for me, but I slid off the bed and his expression fell. "Are you okay? I didn't hurt you, did I?"

I shook my head, flattered he'd asked. "No, but I have to know you better before I let you undress me."

"I'm sorry, Oriana."

"Don't be. I've been living with this for two years now and I've learned what my triggers are." I paused as I unbuttoned my capris. "Or at least, most of them. I haven't had sex with anyone in that time."

He blinked. "What?"

I raised my eyebrows. "Sex. I haven't had it with anyone since my assault." I pushed the denim over my hips, taking my underwear with it. Scott didn't even drop his gaze.

His lovely hard-on wilted as he considered my words and I watched his face, wondering if I'd totally ruined his evening. *Damn, and I didn't even get that orgasm he promised me.* I sighed. I hadn't had sex with another person for two reasons, the first being I didn't really like it after the assault. It had taken me a while to find pleasure in touching my own body again, much less feeling someone else's hands on me.

But the second reason was most people who found out I'd been raped were either repulsed by my past or weren't patient enough to see beyond the triggers. I had to be on top. I had to undress myself. I had to get used to them touching me. None of that "sexy" foreplay for me. That turned off a lot of partners quick.

He stayed silent so long I figured I'd missed the boat to pleasureville. I bent over and grabbed my capris.

"Hey, no worries. I get it. It's hard to have sex with someone as messed up as I am." I stuffed my feet into the bottoms and pulled them up. "Thanks for letting me give you a blowjob. I enjoyed it."

I looked for my top as he surged off the bed, glorious in his nakedness despite his lack of arousal. I loved the lines of his body, how the muscles created interesting mounds and valleys along his bone structure. I loved the scent of his skin and the ink on his arm and back. The flesh appeared a little puckered there, as if he'd been burned, but it fit so perfectly with the man he was. *Too bad I won't be able to sample the rest of him.*

He caught my arm and crowded me up against the wall with his bulk, his hand flat against my forearm without squeezing. I waited for the panic to rise, but instead of fear I felt wanted and protected. *I've lost my mind with this guy.*

"Oriana, I want you so much it makes my chest ache. I've had blue balls for two fuckin' days thinkin' about havin' sex with you." He tipped my face up to meet his gaze. "I'd never thought about what you went through and how hard it would be to come back from it. Hell, it makes me want to find the guy who did this to you and beat the living shit outta him."

I searched Scott's gaze to ascertain the honesty in his eyes. "I wish I could've beaten the shit out of him, too. But no one believed he'd do such a thing. He was a 'pillar of the community' and had too much to lose to do anything so heinous." Bitterness pulled the edges of my lips down.

Scott cupped my face and rubbed them with his thumbs. "I believe you and I want you. And I'll do sex your way anytime you want it, darlin'. You deserve pleasure. I get it from givin' it to you."

I sighed, closing my eyes against the tears threatening to fall. "I have to be on top, Scott. I can't be under you, and you can't take me from behind. It makes me panic. I can't do any rough or fast play. It triggers me into remembering that night. Hell, I'm not even good at letting someone else undress me. I'm really broken."

"You're not broken." He shook his head. "You're

special and you know yourself better than any of the rest of these assholes around here. Even me." He stepped back and tilted his head. "Tell you what. Why don't you take your clothes off again and lie down on the bed? I'd like to run my hands over you. You can watch me the whole time and tell me what feels good and what doesn't, and we'll go from there. Okay?"

I stared at him for a few moments trying to figure out if he was teasing me or not. Who was this guy? What happened to the cocky biker dude?

"You want me to take my clothes off?" At least I understood that much.

"Yeah. And lay on the bed. I'll lie next to you and we'll take it one step at a time." He took another step back and gestured to his bed.

I narrowed my eyes, trying to determine if he was kidding. But his expression remained patient and compassionate, something I never expected out of a guy with the moniker "Scott Free." I blinked and slid my capris off again, trying not to blush while his gaze perused my body. *Why the hell am I feeling shy now?* I shoved the unease down deep and crawled onto the bed, settling where he'd been just a few minutes before.

"Comfy?" Scott grinned as he settled on the bed beside me.

"Kinda. I feel a little weird."

He nodded. "We'll just have to build up the good vibes again. I want you to see me so nothing's a surprise. From what you've told me, you've had enough surprises to last a lifetime. So here's what I'm gonna do." He raised his hand to stroke my midline without touching my breasts. "I'm gonna tell you what I'm doin' while I'm doing it so you can see and feel it at the same time. And if I do something you don't like, you can tell me." His hand stopped above my mound. "Sound good?"

I couldn't help the smirk. "Feels good, too."

"Hell yeah. Let's get this foreplay started." He returned his hand to my collar bones while the other popped his head up. "Your body is fuckin' gorgeous, Oriana. I love how soft your skin is." He trailed his fingers around the curves of my breasts, first the left one then the right.

His touches remained light and sensual, igniting some long-buried arousal I hadn't experienced in years. He watched me watching him, his expression both focused and hopeful. I didn't want to let him down anymore than he wanted to hurt me. The question was, could I relax and enjoy it enough for us both to get our wishes?

I swallowed hard. "I'm sure you've touched a lot of soft-skinned women." I regretted the words as soon as they left my mouth. This wasn't about comparison or his past. This was supposed to be about pleasure, but my asshole analytical side wouldn't let it rest.

"Maybe. I don't really remember. None of them are as important as you right now."

Nice words, but I wondered if he'd forget me just as quickly as he did the others. My arousal cooled and disappointment settled into my gut.

"Hey, where did you go?" He skimmed his fingers up to my face and turned my head toward him.

"Nowhere. I'm still here, just ordinary me. Your current interest."

His eyebrows went up. "My current interest?"

"Yeah, one in a long line of forgettable women you've enjoyed." I shrugged. "I get it. I'm no one special, just the one woman who didn't fall at your feet when you gave her the 'come hither' look."

"Whoa, whoa, whoa." Scott laid his hand over my heart and met my gaze squarely. "You're not "just one in a long line" of women. I'm not claiming to be a monk, but contrary to popular belief I don't screw just anyone." He gave a rueful laugh. "But here's what's good about that. I have a lot of experience, so you're not getting a lover who's an overexcited teenager with no skill. I also know when I see someone worth all my attention and effort. You're definitely that kind of woman."

"You're just saying that because I sucked your cock."

"No, but that sure was a helluva bonus. You're definitely one of the most talented cocksuckers I know." He winked.

"Ew, shut up!" I smacked his chest with the flat of my hand, but I couldn't help the laughter boiling up. "I don't think that's something I'd put on my resume."

"You better not. I don't want to share that talent with any other guy." His gaze settled into deep, erotic intensity. "That's a skill I want to keep all to myself."

I smirked. "You know I'll need lots of practice to keep myself in top condition."

He grinned. "Hell yeah. I'm always available for your workouts."

I laughed and he resumed his stroking of my body with his fingers. He slid them across my belly and along my thigh, making me shiver. I'd never had a guy take the time to do anything more than grope, like selecting a ripe avocado. But Scott seemed to be sensing the textures and forms of my skin. I hadn't expected that kind of sensitivity in a man like him, but I quickly revised my opinion.

When he came back up the inside of my leg, he skirted past the overgrown wedge of pubic hair on my mound. I used to keep it well trimmed so it wouldn't show outside of a bathing suit, but after my assault, it didn't seem worth it anymore. I squirmed with discomfort and his gaze snapped to mine.

"Too much?"

I shook my head with a grimace. "No, I'm just not satisfied with my body."

"Why?" He seemed genuinely perplexed. "It's beautiful. I can tell you're strong because there's muscle here." He grasped my thigh and squeezed gently. "And here." He moved his hand to my biceps. "And here." He trailed his fingers over my belly down to my mound.

"I'm not exactly ripped, Scott." I wriggled at his touches and his hand slipped into my hair. I gasped, but he didn't try to cop a feel.

"You don't have to be 'ripped' to be strong. And I prefer my women to have curves rather than skin-covered skeletons." He still hadn't moved his hand. "You are feminine and curvy and beautiful." He shifted to his knees over my body, his cock and balls hanging between his thighs as he pushed my legs apart. "If you don't mind, I'd like to get a better view of your pussy. That okay with you?"

I thought having a large man crouched over me would scare me, but Scott's gentleness and attention to my needs had dissolved my fears. I nodded and he settled belly-down on the bed between my legs. His shoulders barely fit between them even when he drew his arms under my thighs to wrap around my hips.

"Ah, much better." He grinned up at me before he inhaled deeply. "Damn, you smell good. Sweet and tangy, like a ripe apricot." He licked his lips. "My all-time favorite summer fruit."

"Apricots?"

"Oh yeah." He sighed as he closed his eyes, his face filling with blissful delight. "Sweet enough to make it addicting, but just enough tang to keep it interesting and refreshing. Like you." He met her gaze. "You're sharp like the tang of the apricot, but full of heart and strength to bring out the sweetness." He swept his thumbs through my pubic hair, his gaze hot as he met mine. "Will you let me taste you to see if I'm right?"

His thumbs kept massaging my mound as he waited for me to make a decision, a warm, patient expression on his face. My heart melted in that moment. I suspected he would stop if I told him no, but I craved human touch, particularly of the sexual variety. It helped that I wanted him to do naughty things to me, but I wanted Scott in particular. He was far more than his rough exterior.

Glory, I lo—

I shut the thought down fast before it made me panic. It was too early for such emotions and now wasn't the time. Dredging my voice from somewhere deep in my chest, I nodded.

"Please, Scott. Taste me."

The smile curling his lips was heart-stopping.

Without a word, he dipped his head and kissed my nether lips with exquisite tenderness. I'd never been pleasured between the legs with the same gentleness. All the guys I'd been with before either ate me like a dog gorging itself or avoided my pussy altogether. But Scott took his time, licking and kissing my pussy lips, and I melted onto the bed.

Pleasure surged through me and my orgasm built at lightning speed. It had been so long since someone made an effort to please me, my body had no stamina against his sensual determination. I expected his touches to remind me of the night in the broom closet, but the two events didn't remotely compare. Though Scott wrapped his arms around my hips, I didn't feel held down at all. When he stroked my breasts while his tongue lapped at my pussy, I felt cherished and valued rather than taken.

"Oh my glory, Scott. Oh, oh, oooohhhh!"

My words devolved into little more than sounds as my orgasm crashed over me. Scott hummed his approval as I moaned and writhed, the vibrations sending sweet aftershocks rolling through my body. I whimpered and shook, reveling in the elusive pleasure of my release. I wanted it to last forever, to be strong enough to override the memories of my rape. I wanted to imprint it on my psyche so it would be the first memory I accessed when I thought of sex.

Scott gently lowered my legs and crawled up the bed to lie beside me. He kissed the side of my head and gathered me into his arms, pulling me close.

"Shh, I got you. You're safe, darlin'."

I didn't understand the necessity for his words until I realized my face had grown wet. Tears flooded out of my eyes and down my cheeks without my express okay. Why the hell was I crying?

The question made me analyze the emotions thundering through me. Pleasure, no question, but also amazement, gratitude, relief, and fear. Fear that I'd need more of this kind of pleasure. Fear that Scott would hold it over me as a means to control me and my actions. I'd become his "old lady", his property. Nothing more than a possession to be thrown away when I was no longer interesting or useful.

"Hey, why are you crying?" He rose up to meet my gaze. "I didn't hurt you, did I?"

I shook my head, trying to find words to explain the myriad of thoughts and feelings. But they wouldn't come and the tears wouldn't stop. I let go of the effort to find coherency and turned my face to his chest, wetting his skin with my sorrow.

He didn't ask any more questions. He held me in his arms providing comfort without restriction and let me sob into his chest. I'd never experienced the perfect blending of release and comfort before in my life, and it allowed me to relax for the first time in two years. The last thing I remembered was the scent of masculine safety surrounding me as I fell asleep.

CHAPTER NINE

Scott

"I want to know the mudfucker Oriana Hunter worked for when she was with the FBI." I pushed my way into Neo's lair and crossed my arms over her chest.

"Hello to you, too, Scott." Neo's dry voice reached my ears though he didn't turn around from his terminal. "What's this about now?"

"She told me what happened to her and by whom." My voice was little more than a snarl. "I want to know who he is, where he lives, who he pretends to fuck, what he ate for breakfast the last three days, and the times he takes a shit. I want him now."

Neo sighed. "You know she worked for the FBI, right?"

"Yeah, and?"

"And you take out one of them, you get the entire Federal Bureau of Intimidation breathing down your neck."

I scowled. "I can't believe you'd let a rapey asshole go like this."

Neo's expression darkened. "I'm not letting it go, just

putting it on the back burner until we get shit figured out."

My anger remained, but I took a mental step back. "You're talking about Roy."

"Yeah, shit doesn't add up." Neo turned back to his monitors, clicking on a few things. "I'm pretty sure he didn't go cellphone free while in Denver, but he didn't take the one we have on file. He either turned it off for the whole weekend or left it in the hotel room with Melrose, and that doesn't make any sense."

I frowned as he pulled up a map of Denver with some pretty light blue lines showing the path of Roy's phone. I don't know why Neo picked that color for him. I'd expect shit brown or maybe a dirt gray to represent the jackass, but the blue definitely stood out. The lines ran from our location, squiggled around a little in Fort Collins then made a straight shot to Denver where it stopped. The second line started in Longmont when he turned the phone back on.

"Did he say who he'd been meeting with?" I rubbed my chin as a new idea took form. It was farfetched and so thin as to be anorexic, but there were hints of truth I'd been ignoring.

Neo shrugged. "Yeah, he said he had contracts down there he needed to iron out. But here's the thing. I hacked into security cameras around the usual places he's gone in the past and he never showed up there. Loki sent Attila down to check them out and ask around, but no one had seen him."

Attila was a guy who looked just like a Hungarian barbarian. He even wore hides of various animals he'd killed and skinned. Most were things like deer, elk, and antelope, but he definitely had one coyote hide he sometimes wore as a hat over his long dread-locked hair. If anyone embodied the "badass biker" persona, it was Attila.

"Come on, no one? What about the security cameras in front of the hotel? If we can see which way he went, we can get a clue where to look." I rubbed my chin as a niggling truth tried to get my attention. What was it about Roy that set me off? Until Oriana had arrived, he'd been just another road mate, a guy part of the crew.

Until Oriana arrived.

I blinked. She'd shown up with Melrose and suddenly Roy found places to be that didn't include the compound. Hell, even since he'd been back, he stayed away from the clubhouse at mealtimes and didn't use the rec room that much when he used to be a fixture. What the hell?

"What if…what if he's avoiding Numbers?"

Neo raised his eyebrows. "What?"

I rubbed my chin, the texture of the rough hairs helping me organize my thoughts. "What if he's undercover FBI and he's avoiding Oriana? That would explain why he took off almost as soon as she arrived and why he disappeared in Denver. Hell, it might even explain why he hooked up with Melrose since she was Oriana's "friend." If he's undercover, he might need to avoid a disgraced agent."

"Come on. We'd know if he was an undercover agent. Nobody's that good, especially around Loki."

I shrugged. "Maybe he had a great background put in place. And really, he didn't have to do much but hang around, do what he's told, and collect info. He didn't start acting squirrelly until Oriana, a former FBI agent, was brought in. As I recall, he lit on out of here like his ass was on fire." My gut told me I was right, or at least close, but I had no evidence.

"The problem is I can't tell where he's been unless we find his other phone, assuming he has one."

I shook my head. "Nah, we got two ways to figure it out. Follow the security camera videos to see if we can track where he went, and introduce him to Oriana."

Neo rubbed his own chin. "But if he's FBI, what if he's the guy who raped her?"

Oh shit. I hadn't considered that. On the other hand, it would give me the opportunity to kick the shit out of both

Roy the asshole and the monster who'd hurt Oriana all at once. But it was it worth it to make her face him again?

"There's an easy way to figure that shit out." I pointed at the screens. "Bring up the man who was her supervisor while she worked there. See if you can find his ID card or a picture of him. That'll tell us if he's Roy or not."

Neo ground his teeth, but he brought up Oriana's file. Before he opened it, he looked around his lair to make sure we were alone before tapping the keys to open the icon.

Oriana's face and stats filled the screen. She'd taken a great ID photo in a smart blue suit with a v-necked white shirt underneath. Her hair had been pulled back behind her head and her startling hazel eyes stared boldly at the camera. She wore a Mona Lisa smile as if she knew something no one else did. *Where did that woman go?* When I'd met her, the bold smile had disappeared to be replaced by a wary, watchful mask that showed very little.

I need to help her find her Mona Lisa smile again.

"Here it is." Neo's voice interrupted my perusal of her image. "It says her supervisory agent was a guy named Dirk Hopkins." His fingers flew over the keys and an image showed up on another monitor. "According to the website, he's still an active agent."

I scowled. "Oriana said he kept his job while she was chased out of hers."

I studied the image of the man in front of me. He reminded me of a smooth, confident con-artist. His half-smile failed to reach the blue eyes and the clean-shaven cleft chin made me want to mar the masculine good-looks. The image projected a sense of what the All-American boy-next-door would look like if he grew up. Perfect, handsome, and unreproachable.

Except I know you're a rapist.

"So he's not Roy." Roy had pale blue eyes and Teutonic features with a pinched mouth. "But it doesn't mean Roy's not undercover FBI. I think we need to find out where he went, at least as far as the cameras can tell us."

"Yeah, well, that's gonna take a while. It's four a.m. Go get some sleep. Hell, go back to bed with Numbers. She gave you a helluva good ride, didn't she?"

Actually, I'd given her one of the best orgasms and then made her cry. I wasn't sure the crying was such a good thing, but she'd turned to me and fallen asleep in my arms. I counted that as a win.

"A gentleman doesn't kiss and tell."

Neo snorted. "Since when are you any kind of gentleman?"

Since I met Oriana. "Let's just say I hold few things sacred and my time with Numbers is one of them."

Neo raised his eyebrows and blinked a couple of times. "Okay. Got it. You gonna put a property tag on her?"

I barked a laugh. "It's a little early to do that. We're just having a good time." But somewhere in my gut I knew it was a lie. "Besides, I'm pretty sure she won't let me. She's not one to be 'owned.'"

Neo nodded. "Yeah, she's definitely not my type. Too analytical."

"Really? Analytical is a problem for you, the guy who sits in a dark room all day and night, following little incomprehensible codes?" I chuckled. "You're messed up, man."

"No argument here." Neo turned back to his monitors. "I'll text you if I find anything interesting."

"Thanks."

I headed back out of his lair and looked around the clubhouse. Most of the lights were off and dark shapes could be found on the arm chairs and couches. I remembered times when I'd been too drunk to drive anywhere and didn't have my own cabin onsite. I'd crashed on those couches and hoped no one would throw up on me some time during the night. We now had barracks for the Scooters and any honeys sticking around, but people still slept in the main room.

I skirted past them, heading for my cabin and Oriana's gorgeous body. Making love with her had been an experience that compared with nothing else in my life. She'd been the perfect blend of sensual, erotic, bold, and innocent. Oh, she wasn't a virgin, but knowing her background included rape, her response to my touches had been gratifying. She guarded herself and kept most people at bay. Hell, it didn't surprise me given all the people who'd lied to her. Her supervisor, the FBI, Melrose, and me.

I stopped in front of my cabin's door, my gut sinking. I hadn't lied to her, really. I just hadn't clarified something she'd talked about. I paused at the cabin's door.

Loki's not going to let her go.

My gut did funny things at that thought. On the one hand, that was awesome. I'd be able to be with Oriana a lot more, maybe even solidify our fling into something more permanent so I could make her my old lady. But on the other hand, she'd made it clear she wouldn't like being a prisoner, told where she could go and when. I suspected she knew that on some level, but she would be furious when she found out for sure.

I need to tell her, to correct her misconception, but I wanted to do that as much as I wanted to drive nails through my feet. Why couldn't I have more time with Oriana and convince her to stay on her own? Then I wouldn't have to tell her she had no choice.

I sighed and leaned my forehead against the door. Maybe that was the best way to do it. Court her, seduce her with kindness and sex, and convince her to choose staying with the Concrete Angels for good. Then I wouldn't have to tell her she couldn't leave.

Some of my tension released and I opened the door to my cabin, navigating through the darkness with ease. I shucked my clothes as soon as I got into the bedroom, but paused before I crawled into the bed.

Oriana slept soundly, her even breathing filling the room with a gentle rhythm. More of the tension in my shoulders melted away. *I could fuckin' get used to this.* What would it be like to have a woman waiting in bed for me? My cock saluted the idea, but not as much as the heart in my chest. I wanted Oriana. I wanted her to be there, to tease me, laugh with me, and let me love her. The question was, how did I get her to want that, too?

I stripped down to nothing and crawled into bed with my beautiful lover. She actually sighed and snuggled back against my chest as I wrapped my arms around her. *That's a good sign.* I'd take the small victory and hope for more.

CHAPTER TEN

Oriana

I rolled my head on my neck and rubbed my eyes with my hands. Damn, the numbers had started to run together and I wanted a break. *You just want to spend more time with Scott between your legs.* Yeah, okay, after a steady diet of hot sex with the cocky biker for the last four days and nights, I'd become a bit of an addict. I liked feeling good after sex. I liked the way he looked at me and the soft touches he gave when no one was looking.

Hell, he did that when everyone was looking, too.

And it didn't bother me. I liked the attention and the effort. He was the only man who'd ever taken the time to make sure I was enjoying myself when it came to sexual pleasure. It was like finding a unicorn and I was all about his "horn."

But you're not going to get out of here if you don't solve Loki's problem.

I groaned and focused on the data in front of me again. I was close to figuring out where the money had gone and who'd put it there, but the pattern still eluded me. To be brutally honest, Loki's system was as crazy as the leader himself. *Reminds me of the frickin' God of Mischief.* Not many people would be able to ferret out the ways the money came in and where it went just by looking at his books. Most of it looked like a pile of cooked spaghetti.

After spending all this time on it, though, I'd made enough connections to organize it a bit better. It still would take an expert in forensic accounting to figure it out, but at least the lines were straight, now. I hadn't asked Loki if he wanted his system to change, but this new organization allowed me to see where things were getting 'misplaced' and prevent it from happening in the future.

I just couldn't see who'd done it in the first place.

"Okay, Hunter. You know how this goes. Follow the money." Hearing my own voice helped me regroup, but I still got up from my chair and headed for the kitchenette to get something to drink. "Yeah, that's what I've been doing. If Loki's money wasn't all over the place, it's would be easier to follow."

I poured myself some lemonade as I thought over the problem, letting my gaze unfocus. It had gotten hot the last couple of days and even the monsoonal rains hadn't done much more than spit on us. The only positive was the heat kept me glued to my chair in front of the laptop.

Follow the money. Easier to follow.

I repeated the words in my head as I headed back to my chair, settling into it with a thump. That hadn't been working even though it seemed logical.

But Loki isn't logical. I blinked. "No, he isn't. What if it isn't the money I need to follow?"

I brought up the financial records and scanned them again. I knew where the money had been skimmed and when, now. I even knew the amounts, but the person doing it had remained elusive. I narrowed my eyes. *Who was present each time one of the transactions go wonky?*

I snorted at my "technical term" and started a list of

names for each transaction. After a while, two names stood out. Orion and Huntsman. When I'd first read them, I thought they were road names, the nicknames the members of the Concrete Angels earned for themselves. But Michael had given her their official membership list, including any contacts involved in their money ventures, and neither Orion or Huntsman came up.

"So, who are you, really?"

I frowned as I sat back in my chair, crossing my arms over my chest. Whoever they were, they'd been smart when it came to skimming money until recently. They'd been doing it for a while from what I could see, taking small amounts that wouldn't be noticed. But more recently, they'd gotten greedy and taken larger sums, probably hoping the disorganization would hide it. *Not anymore.* But who the hell would be stupid enough to take from their own crew?

"Ugh!" I rubbed my eyes with the heels of my hands as someone knocked on my cabin door. "What?"

Scott poked his head in, eyebrows raised. "Everything okay in here? I brought a snack of fresh peaches from the farmer's market." He held up a plate of sliced peaches.

"You sliced them for me?" I tilted my head as he stepped through the door and closed it behind him.

"Yeah, well, no. Dollhouse did the slicing, but I brought them. That should count for something, right?" He grinned as he brought them to the table. "How's it goin'?"

"Good. I've figured out when, where, and how much money has been embezzled from the Concrete Angels."

"Fan-fucking-tastic, Numbers." He grinned, but it faded when all I did was nod. "Isn't that enough to figure out who did it?"

I sighed and shook my head. "No, unfortunately. Or rather, yeah with a catch."

"What's the catch?"

"I've figured out a couple of names, but they're

aliases. And I don't know who they belong to." I reached for a slice of fruit with a grimace. "You don't happen to know who Orion and the Huntsman are, do you?"

Scott frowned and shook his head. "Nope. That doesn't sound familiar. But I might be able to narrow it down for you."

"Really?" Relief skittered across my shoulders. "How?"

He scooted his chair over to mine so he could see the screen. "Loki keeps our organization kinda loose. None of us knows all the business of the other members. That way if we ever get caught or hounded by the cops—"

"Or the FBI," I added dryly.

"—we can't give up everything. But, a few of us, me included, know more than the average member." He winked. "I've been here longer than a lot of the guys, and I've gotten to know who some of their contacts are. If you can show me where the money was skimmed and who Orion and the Huntsman were meeting at the time, I might be able to skirt the aliases."

"Okay. You better settle in, Alice, because this rabbit hole gets gnarly."

"As long as you got a caterpillar smokin' the good stuff, I'm sure it'll be fine." He stretched his hands in front of him, cracking the knuckles. "Just remember, we're all mad here."

I laughed and winked before we dug into the mass of data and pathways. I didn't show him everything in Loki's financial world, but I did show him the places where Orion or the Huntsman showed up. It took us well over two hours, but with Scott helping, it became clear that Orion and the Huntsman were the same person.

"Duh." I thumped my forehead with the heel of my palm. "Orion *is* the Huntsman in Greek lore. I should've picked up on that. The question is, who is he?"

I shot a look at Scott, who'd gone really quiet. Eerily

so. "Scott?"

He sat staring at the screen, his jaw set. "We need to go talk to Loki."

"Okay, but why? Have you figured out who the embezzler is?"

"Yeah. Bring your laptop so you can show him and Neo." He got up.

"Right now?" I scrambled to my feet as unease slid through me.

"Right fuckin' now." Anger threaded through his voice and his hands clenched into fists.

I saved the files I had open and put the laptop to sleep before shoving my feet into my shoes. I'd seen Scott angry before, but not furious like this. I shivered, glad I wasn't the subject of his fury. I could defend myself against most of the members of the Concrete Angels, but that didn't mean I wanted to get into it with them, least of all Scott.

I grabbed the laptop and my keys as Scott ushered me out the door. He barely waited for me to lock my cabin before he hustled me into the clubhouse, his face a mask of fury. Whatever he'd figured out pissed him off something good, and I didn't have a clue what it was. I mean, yeah, I knew embezzlement was a betrayal of trust and good faith, but this seemed more personal.

We didn't say anything to anyone as we headed back to Loki's office, but Michael caught Scott's furious expression and rose to follow us. We all reached the door to the office at the same time.

"What's going on, Scott?"

"We got a federal rat in our house." Scott scowled as he knocked on the door.

Michael's eyes widened and he shot a look at me. "We already knew Oriana was former FBI."

Scott growled. "Not her. Someone else. Someone I shoulda known."

Loki's voice called us to come in and we stepped

across the threshold. I don't know what I was expecting, but a study filled with bookshelves and elegant but rough-hewn furniture wasn't it. It looked like a place you'd meet a Sheik or King for a private audience, and I had the sense I'd been granted a rare privilege to be ushered inside.

Loki looked up from the book he'd been reading with his feet propped up on an ornate, cushioned ottoman, and nodded to us.

"Michael, Scott, Ms. Hunter. What brings you to my office?"

"We found the mudfucker who's been stealing from us." Scott spat the words in a low roar.

"This is good news, though, *ja*?" He set the book aside and gestured to one of the low tables in front of the bookshelves. "Come show me what you've found, Oriana."

I swallowed hard. "Scott identified him. I just found his tracks."

Loki nodded. "I'm sure. But without those tracks, Scott wouldn't know the name. Start at the beginning and walk me through it, *ja*?"

I took a deep breath and blew it out as I opened my laptop. "Okay."

I showed him how I'd untangled his money streams and how I followed the transactions. I also showed him how I'd changed the organization so he or another accountant could keep things straight from now on. I eyed him as I explained, but instead of being angry at my changes, he nodded with approval. *Thank the Goddess for that.* The last thing I wanted to do was piss off the client.

"Once I figured out where the money was being taken, I cross referenced the incidences with who seemed to show up. And I got two names." He shot a look at Scott, but his fury hadn't changed. "Orion and the Huntsman. I didn't get the reference until Scott took a look at it with me. Once we discovered the two aliases were the same person, Scott said we needed to bring it to you."

Loki nodded. "Who is Orion the Huntsman, Scott?"

"It's Roy." The growl in Scott's voice made me shiver with unease. "I knew there was somethin' wrong with him, but this just proves it."

Loki narrowed his eyes. "How are you sure?"

"When Oriana said the same names kept coming up on the hinky transactions, I took a look where they happened. I recognized the names of the contacts as those belonging to Roy's accounts." He shook his head. "I totally shoulda known it was him."

"Oh? Why is that?" Michael raised his eyebrows.

"Because I got to thinkin' about that trip Roy took to Denver and how he went all over town without his cellphone or girlfriend. He said he was meetin' contacts, but Attila checked and none of his usual contacts saw him that weekend." Scott scowled and shrugged. "So I had Neo check up on him."

"Really?" Loki gave a half-smile that made the hairs stand up on my neck. "Please call him in here. I want to hear his account."

Scott texted our computer guru as Loki shifted his attention back to me. "This is good work, Ms. Hunter. And I like your organization of the financial records. It will make it easier to spot thieves before they take too much." He tilted his head. "How much did Roy get, anyway?"

I bit my bottom lip. "Three million, four hundred, seventy-six thousand, two hundred and forty-five dollars and eighty-one cents."

Anger glittered in his eyes, but he snorted with laughter. "You could've rounded up."

I shook my head. "I've found it's best to be honest and accurate when it comes to money."

He smiled. "You're wiser than your years, Ms. Hunter."

"Thank you, sir."

Neo picked that moment to knock and enter. "You

called me?"

"*Ja.* Shut the door, Neo."

The dark-haired man took in our little tableau as he closed the door behind him. "What's up?"

"Scott says you tracked Roy in Denver. What did you find out?"

Neo's expression darkened with anger, but his voice remained steady. "Scott had the bright idea to use security cameras in the area of the hotel to track where Roy went when the cellphone didn't pan out. It took a little while, but after a circuitous route, he ended up in a bar in Aurora."

"That's not really news. Roy goes to lots of bars to make deals." Michael crossed his arms over his chest. "What makes this one so special?"

"Let me show you." Neo had brought his own laptop and pulled up the surveillance records he had from tracking Roy. "He never leaves. See?"

The security footage from a bank ATM across the street showed Roy pulling up into the bar's parking lot, parking his bike in an out-of-the way space at the back of the lot, and going inside.

"I know that doesn't look like much, but his bike stays there for the next three days without moving." Neo showed the time stamps on the video he'd accessed. "That seemed weird so I went back and hacked into the bar's security system. He didn't talk to or sit with anyone at the bar, but he headed for the bathroom about an hour in and didn't come out of there, either. I found the bar has a security camera out the back and that's when I hit pay dirt."

He tapped a few keys and sat back to show us the footage. The man I assumed was Roy appeared with his back to the camera. It took me a moment but I could read his name on the cut's patch along with the Concrete Angels' emblem. He strode to a nondescript sedan parked in the camera's view, opened the door, and slid inside after taking one last look toward the bar.

"Wait, stop. Go back." Unease settled into my gut as Neo raised his eyebrows but rewound the footage. "There. Can you do anything to enhance the image when he turns and faces the camera? I need to see his face."

"What is it, Oriana?" Scott's brows were low but he sounded more curious than angry.

I didn't answer as Neo's fingers flew over the keyboard, working his computer magic while we waited. *Please don't be right. Please be a trick of the light.* But my stomach sank and curdled as the image became clearer. The pixels remained a little fuzzy, but I knew that face and those eyes.

"Oh glory." I stepped back and hugged my arms around myself.

Scott stepped up next to me, all the anger replaced by concern in his expression. "What, Oriana? What do you see?"

I met his gaze, his green eyes filled with compassion and concern. I didn't want to lose that, or the connection I'd made with him. I didn't want to ruin the camaraderie I'd built with Neo, Michael, Dollhouse, Karma, and the others in the Concrete Angels. But when they found out who Roy really was, all that would be ashes. His girlfriend was my supposed friend. They'd only heard about me through Roy and her. Hell, Roy had even used a version of my name as his aliases. And I'd formerly worked for his current employer.

"Come on, darlin'. What do you see?"

I swallowed hard. "I know him. I know Roy. He works for the FBI."

CHAPTER ELEVEN

Scott

I knew it!

That's the first thought that roared through my head. I knew Roy was undercover FBI, and that explained why he was avoiding Oriana while she was here. He didn't want her to recognize him.

"Who is he really, Oriana?" Michael's gaze met mine over her head.

"His name is Arnold Eisenburg. I don't know what department he worked in, but..." She trailed off and swallowed hard, all the blood leaving her face. "H-he was good friends...with..."

She swallowed again and clenched her hands into fists as she closed her eyes, shaking her head. I recognized that reaction and stepped forward to grasp her fists in my hands, holding them loosely.

"I got you, Oriana. I'm here. You're safe with the Concrete Angels." I hoped that was true. I hoped Loki wouldn't see the connections between her and Roy, no matter how tenuous. "Breathe. No one can touch you.

You're in Loki's office. Roy can't get you here. You're safe."

I kept my voice even and massaged her hands with my thumbs, hoping she wouldn't completely succumb to a PTSD episode. She kept shaking her head, her breath coming in short pants. She made some noises and at first, I thought she was moaning, but when I dipped my head, I could make out words.

"No, no. How did he find me? Does he know? Did they both know? Did Mel know? Why won't he leave me alone? I walked away. I lost everything. Why won't he leave me alone?"

I looked up at Michael and shook my head, but I kept rubbing her hands in hopes I'd get through to her. He took a few steps closer and rested his hands on her shoulders. She jumped at first but calmed as a soft, soothing hum filled the air. My own heartbeat slowed and my anger dissipated as Michael closed his eyes and bowed his head. A glow filled the room, making the space seem warmer, softer, a place of comfort.

Oriana's tension gradually reduced and so did mine, as if we'd become connected. I didn't like it when she was afraid. I'd do my damnedest to make sure she wasn't afraid again. As long as she stayed with me, I'd protect her.

Oriana stopped shaking her head and her breathing returned to normal. So had the humming and light. In fact, I wondered if I'd imagined it as she took a deep breath and opened her eyes, meeting mine.

"Arnold Eisenburg was good friends with my rapist, Dirk Hopkins. If Arnold is undercover here in the Concrete Angels, Dirk knows about me. And if he comes near me again, I'm gonna shoot him. Are we clear?"

Her steady, firm statement made my lips curl in a smile. "Yes, ma'am."

"Good." She turned her attention to Loki. "I have nothing to do with Arnold or Roy or whoever he is. Mel befriended me a little under a year ago and she never mentioned that her boyfriend was FBI. She just called him Roy and said he was with the Concrete Angels. But I know Arnold was part of the Old Boy's club at the Denver office of the FBI and he helped discredit me." Fury rippled across her face for a moment before it sank into her impassive mask. "If I see him, I'm liable to shoot him, too."

Loki grinned. "I just might let you do that, Ms. Hunter. But in the meantime, we first have to figure out where the money has gone and how to get it back before we kill him, *ja*?"

"That I can help you with." Oriana spun to her laptop and started tapping on the keys. "I know where it went, but I don't have any way to get into the accounts."

"How many accounts are we talkin' here?" I stood behind her to get a nice view of her ass and to look over her shoulder. It was a guy thing and she had a fantastic ass.

"Eight." She clicked on a few windows and opened them up before spinning the screen toward Loki. "They're under some variation of Huntsman or Orion, scattered across several banks in Europe and the Cayman Islands. Like I said, I found them and their amounts, but can't see the activity within them."

Loki smiled. "That's Neo's job. He'll get into them to recover our money."

She nodded. "Then, I guess that's it. I'll make sure Neo has all the information that I found and you understand how the system works so you can keep track of your funds. And I'll be on my way."

I frowned. "On your way?"

"Yeah." She nodded as she made sure the files were in order. "My contract has concluded. I did what y'all asked and now it's time for me to go home."

I shot a look at Michael and Neo. Both men had stilled, their expressions uneasy. Loki, however, looked subtly amused. Oriana's eyes narrowed.

"I *am* going home. We both signed a contract, in blood no less." She raised her chin. "We all agreed."

Loki nodded as he rose to his feet, his half-amused look remaining. "We did agree, but that was before you found our money, reorganized our financial holdings and income streams, and got a good look at where the money comes from." He spread his hands in a helpless gesture. "You see why it would be dangerous to allow you to leave. I cannot have someone with that much knowledge of my enterprises walking around where just anyone could get to you."

"I'm bound by the accountant-client privilege where I can't share secrets without serious repercussions." She shook her head, her expression set. "The contract *you* signed says I'm free to go."

"You should've read it more carefully, Ms. Hunter."

"I did read it carefully. I was there when it was written."

"Ah, but it says you can only go if you cannot reveal the financial secrets of the Concrete Angels."

"And I won't."

"It didn't say "will not," it said "can not." Which means you're still capable of revealing the secrets." He tilted is head with that infuriating half-smile that always pissed me off when it was aimed at me. "As I see it there are only two ways you "can not" reveal our finances. Either you stay with the Concrete Angels, or you die. The choice is yours."

Panic and protest roared through me, coming out in a growl. There was no way in hell I'd let Loki kill Oriana, national Prez of our organization or not. Oriana was my woman, someone I protected, and killing her was out of the question as far as I was concerned.

"No. No, no, no. This isn't how this is supposed to work. We had a deal." Oriana's hands tightened into fists.

"And we still do. No clause in this contract has been

broken." Loki paused and his gaze slid over to me with that damnable half-smile. "Unless you consider your activities with Scott constitute unwanted molestation, though I'd argue you consented with abandon."

She blushed, but I didn't think it was from embarrassment. Her fury rolled through the room like a sixty-mile-an-hour wind gust as she leveled her gaze on me. I took a step back despite her smaller stature. This woman wasn't someone I'd willingly cross.

"You set this up, didn't you, Scott?" She snarled the words though she hadn't moved. "You kept hinting about me staying, but you never once said I couldn't go. Not once. You lied to me."

"Oriana—"

"I don't need to hear anything from you, Michael." She threw her furious gaze at him. "You do this big thing about family and loyalty and belonging. But you know what's most important about all those things? Honesty. Brutal sometimes, even heartbreaking, but still complete honesty. And you gave me nothing of that."

She swung back to Loki. "I don't choose death." She packed up her laptop and headed for the door of his office, totally ignoring me.

"Oriana, wait." I took a few steps toward her, but I wasn't stupid enough to grab her arm as she rounded on me.

"Stay the fuck away from me, Scott."

"I never lied to you."

"Stop." She held up her free hand. "Don't hand me the 'omission of full truth' argument. That's a cop-out and you know it. You could've been honest. You could've told me I was stuck here forever, but you were too busy charming your way into my bed. Congratulations, you got what you wanted. Hoped you enjoyed it." She shook her head, the corners of her mouth pulling down as if she fought not to cry. "That's all you'll ever get from me."

A soft sob made her breath catch and damn near gutted me. "Goddess-damned Hotel California." She yanked the door open and was gone.

Three pairs of eyes landed on me and I mentally cringed. I didn't need to look to know Michael handed me compassion, Neo offered pity, and Loki slapped me with avid amusement. The bastard loved to see people struggle.

The problem was, I didn't know what to do. Oriana was right that I hadn't told her everything, or made it clear that she'd missed something. And I had charmed my way into her bed, but not ensure the unwanted attention clause. I wanted her, all of her, as she was, and I didn't want her to leave.

Now she'd stay, but I ended up farther away than if she'd gone back to her apartment in Fort Collins.

"Hey, Scott, it'll be okay. Just give her a chance to calm down." Michael gave me a hesitant smile.

"Shut up, Michael. If you think that, then you don't know Oriana very well." I shook my head. "She doesn't forgive liars who betray her trust. And I've done both." I headed for the door.

"Where are you going?" Loki still wore the damn smirk.

"To get a fuckin' drink." I'd need at least a five gallon bucket to drown the pain ripping through my chest, and I wasn't sure that'd be enough.

****

Oriana

I slammed my cabin door and locked it. I wanted to throw the laptop against the wall, but even if it wasn't technically mine, I didn't destroy property.

Oh yeah, Hunter? Still fucking following the rules?

The inner voice infuriated me more. Here I was

because I'd signed a contract that I'd thought Loki would adhere to. And he had, after a fashion. No one could reasonably expect he'd weasel out of it on the *other* definition of can. I certainly hadn't, but then I didn't think his name was anything more than a nickname.

Fuck that. He acts like the goddess-damned God of Mischief for real.

A shiver slithered up my spine at that thought. *What if...?* I snorted and shook my head, but the unease remained. It didn't matter really. I was stuck here.

"I told you, Melinda! I TOLD YOU!" I roared the words into the silence of my cabin. "It's mudfucking Hotel California, a thrice-damned cult!"

I didn't feel better knowing I was right. I'd signed the contract with the wording that allowed Loki to keep me here. Of course, if I could find a lawyer, they could argue for reasonable expectation or something like that, but he wouldn't let me leave to get one.

Still following the rules.

Damn right I was. Just because the Concrete Angels had no honor or integrity didn't mean I followed right along. But my lofty morals and beliefs amounted to less than a hill of beans in my predicament. I threw myself into the little loveseat in my living room and drew my knees up to my chest.

I had to come up with a plan. How the hell was I going to get out of this? Technically, Loki had me by the short hairs. He said I was physically able—or was that fiscally able?—to pass on his financial secrets. But that wasn't truly the case without the laptop that sat on the table. I shot a look over to the offending machine.

Only the pathways and links on the computer made me capable of knowing their secrets. If I could show him I didn't have possession of the laptop, I could weasel my own way out of the contract. It was a technicality, but that's how he'd set up the game, and two could play that way.

All of which was only to keep my mind off of Scott and his betrayal, his lying by omission. Just thinking about him made my stomach contract like someone had stabbed me in the chest. Hell, being shot would feel better.

All the men who'd shown interest in me, romantically or otherwise, had betrayed me in one way or another. I didn't know why I'd thought Scott might have been different. Maybe it was because the other men I'd been with had been hiding behind a respectable image. Scott had sauntered in with his cocky biker persona and I thought that would clear him to be honest.

I guess it just goes to prove when someone tells you who they are, believe them.

I rested my head on my knees and let the tears out. I'd wanted to believe in Scott. I'd gotten used to being with him, sharing the space and meals. And I'd actually liked the sex. I didn't expect to like sex ever again after my rape, but Scott proved me wrong.

That wasn't the only thing I was wrong about him.

I let myself cry for a while, letting the hurt sift through me. I should've known better than to believe Scott when he said he'd have my back. The club came first, as I'd known it would, and he took the path of least resistance.

Least resistance.

Maybe that's what I needed to do, too. Loki required me to stay, but the contract only covered the project of Roy's embezzlement. I'd finished it, solved his problem. I couldn't leave the compound, but I didn't have to do anything more for the Concrete Angels. I could eat, live, lounge around, and do nothing without breaking my contract. And I'd give the laptop back to Neo so I couldn't actually pass on the financial secrets of the club.

The path of least resistance. That would be me.

Except it sounded fucking boring. I wondered which of us would get annoyed with the arrangement first. My tears slowed though the pain remained, and I slowly uncurled before my body locked up that way.

Thunder rumbled outside and I shot a look out the window. Storm clouds had gathered while I moped and it sounded like the rain would start soon. The weather seemed to be mimicking my mood. I rose and headed for my kitchenette to start some tea.

As I waited for it to boil, my thoughts drifted toward Roy/Arnold and how long he'd been undercover in the Concrete Angels. His assignment had to have started after I left the FBI because I'd periodically saw him with Dirk while I worked there. They were good buddies and Arnold had vouched for Dirk's character after I went to H.R. New anger kindled in my chest as the rain pounded on the windows.

Arnold made sure I was discredited. *It would've been unkind to not return the favor.* My dark humor only made me smile. But if I recognized him, he probably recognized me the moment I stepped onto the compound. Which meant if he left the compound while I'd been here, he'd most likely reported my presence to his handler and Dirk.

The old fear crept up and damn near strangled me. I'd packed my shit and left Denver after I quit the FBI. I'd closed all my social media accounts, cut off contact with mutual friends, and disappeared for a while. The FBI had given me a severance package as if to assuage a guilty conscience, and I lived on that for six months before I was able to start my modest at-home accounting business. No one seemed to be looking for me and I slowly relaxed my concern for retribution.

But if Arnold had told Dirk I was here with the Concrete Angels, he'd know where to find me.

Don't be ridiculous, Hunter. He'd need a legitimate reason to come here and a warrant.

The kettle whistled and I pulled it off the stove, my mind sifting through possibilities. Would he bother after all this time? It'd been more than two years, and I'd only done the minimum disappearing act. I'm sure the FBI kept tabs on me after I left just to make sure I didn't cause more trouble for one of its golden sons. He could've dipped into the records to find me.

My gut told me I needed to be prepared, even if I couldn't think of a logical reason why Dirk would waste the time. And if he made the effort, he might concoct an excuse to come up to the compound with the FBI in tow. He could choose anything, and Arnold probably supplied him with suggestions.

Drug lab. Weapons cache. Money laundering. The possibilities were vast. Most judges would believe a highly decorated and respected agent's probable cause allegations. It wouldn't take Dirk and Arnold long to plan a raid.

The question was, did I tell my hosts about it before it happened, or did I let them get caught with their pants down? *Gonna follow the rules again, Hunter? Or are you gonna fuck up the Old Boys club's victory?* Actually it came down to who did I want to fuck over most, the Concrete Angels or the FBI?

"That's a damn good question."

I poured my tea as I considered, both groups deserving of my ire. But the FBI owed me big time, whereas my situation with the Concrete Angels was my own fault. The FBI deserved a good fucking-over.

I grabbed my phone and punched in Michael's number, hitting send.

"Hello, Oriana. Are you all right?"

"Just peachy. Listen, more than likely Roy's told his handler about me and figures I've recognized him. I suspect he knows his cover has been blown and the FBI will stage a raid on the compound after his years of data gathering." I pulled the teabag out of my cup. "If you have anything you don't want the Feds to see, I suggest you get rid of it now. I don't know how much time you have before they show up here."

There was a short silence on the other end of the phone. "Thank you. Why are you telling me this, if I may ask?"

"Because I know how the FBI works and because they fucking hung me out to dry by defending the man who raped me. I think they should get used to being wrong." I swung my gaze around the room. "Oh, and tell Neo to come get his fucking laptop."

I hung up before Michael could say anything else and took my tea in to the bedroom to drink while I turned my brain off by binge-watching a show about the devil falling in love with a homicide detective.

Yeah, like that would happen. About as probable as a cocky biker falling for a nerdy number cruncher. I ignored the tears sliding down my cheeks as I turned on the show.

CHAPTER TWELVE

Scott

Life sucked. Not only did I have the hangover from hell, but Oriana had stopped speaking to me. She wouldn't answer the phone or texts or her door. She hadn't even come into the clubhouse for dinner the first night or meals the next few days. And when she called to let us know the FBI would be showing up, she'd called fucking Michael instead of me. That one hurt the most. She trusted Schnoz more than she trusted me.

With damn good reason, jackass.

She'd warned me when we first talked that I'd choose the club over her, and it looked that way when I did nothing about Loki's interpretation of her contract. But I'd been hoping the contract would become moot because I'd convinced her to stay. That's why I hadn't bothered to tell her of the likelihood she'd be stuck here.

But I hadn't convinced her. I needed more time. Time I wasn't likely to get now.

I chugged some coffee in hopes it would stop the pounding in my head and staggered around my room to find cleanish clothes. It looked like a bomb had gone off and I knew I needed to do laundry, but I didn't really give a shit. My body ached, but not as much as my heart, a heart I hadn't known I had.

I threw on a T-shirt and jerked on my jeans, the denim stiff with sweat and vomit. *Nice. I'm not gonna win any cleanliness awards.* The filth disgusted me and I stripped them off again as I searched for my laundry shorts. I only wore them when there was nothing else. I tossed all the clothes I could find into my laundry basket and headed for the door. I might as well do chores while I felt like shit.

My phone rang and I scanned the caller ID as I headed out the door. *Michael.* Why the hell was he calling me?

"What?" I barked, making some of the Scooters jump and scramble out of my way.

"Good morning to you, too, Sunshine. Feeling a little grumpy this morning?"

"Fuck you. Whadya want, Michael? I got shit to do."

"Right. We've got all the contraband moved out of the compound, but the concern is the warehouses Roy knows about."

Fuck. Roy had been here at least two years and he'd become a useful member of the club. He'd gone to a lot of our storage spaces.

"Do we know how many he's been to?"

"Yeah, Neo's got records, but that's a shit-ton of stuff to move. Half of them are cleared, but we still have three more to empty. One of them's in Fort Collins. Near Oriana's apartment."

"No!" I shoved open the laundry room door and slammed the basket down on a washer. "No fuckin' way. I'm not breaking into her apartment to bring her stuff. She already hates me. I'm not making it worse."

"She doesn't hate you, Scott. She's just angry."

"Gee, I wonder why that is? Maybe because Loki screwed her over and I didn't do anything about it?" I shook my head and shoved clothes into the washer. "I'm not breaking into her place."

"I didn't expect you to break in, dumbass. I expected you to take her with you into Fort Collins so she can get her own stuff. Help her furnish her cabin with her own things."

I snorted as I pressed start on the machine. "Oh yeah, that'll make her feel better. I'm helping her get her stuff to make her incarceration better. Nice."

"Yeah…" Michael sighed on the other end of the phone. "I can't fix that, yet. But how about we work on your end of the relationship? Then at least the ride to Fort Collins won't be too bad."

I rolled my eyes. I was going to Fort Collins with or without Oriana. I didn't think "with" would happen. "Yeah, good luck with that. I don't know what to say if she'll even talk to me."

"Here, let me help you. Begin with "I'm sorry." Continue with "Please forgive me." And possibly add, "What can I do to make it up to you?" That should at least get the ball rolling."

"Fuck you."

"No, you want to fuck her, but you have to first make amends." Michael managed to still sound amused even when I came across as stupid.

"No, I don't want to fuck her. I want to make love with her for the rest of my life."

A short silence echoed through the phone.

"Do you?" All amusement left his voice. "Then you need to talk to her. You need to make her understand she's your priority and the first one you'll stand with. Even against your friends."

"I know. But I signed a blood oath of loyalty to Loki. When he screwed her over, I didn't know what to say."

"Why didn't you tell her you suspected she wouldn't be able to leave when you had the chance?"

I scowled at my feet and rubbed the back of my neck.

"I dunno. I guess I thought I could convince her to stay before it reached that point. I should've said something."

"If you had, it wouldn't have been betraying Loki, you know. And she probably would've been able to deal with it better than just having it dumped on her like that."

"Fuck, yeah, I know. Hindsight's twenty-twenty." I sighed and shook my head. "I just don't want to lose her over something so stupid."

"So talk to her."

"She won't talk to me!"

"Texting doesn't count, mate." Exasperation rumbled into my ear. "Take her with you to Fort Collins. Talk to her even if she doesn't talk back. Glory, tell her how you feel, at least. She deserves to know, especially if she's gonna be stuck around you for a while."

"Why does she deserve to know? She doesn't want to hear it."

Michael took a deep breath as if trying for patience. "Don't be stupid, Scott. She's angry, but she's always been honest with you. Try being honest, and frankly, vulnerable with her. Extend a little of that trust you wanted from her."

I groaned and rubbed my face with one hand. "Fine. Give me an hour. I gotta clean some clothes or I'm going to smell like a nasty-ass sweat shop. Get the guys started on the warehouse and I'll be there as soon as I can."

"Got it. I'll have van ready for you."

"Oh, come on. The van? I'll look like a fuckin' soccer dad."

"How else are you gonna carry her stuff, you stupid git? She might want to take a lot. Speaking of which, take the Bug Detector with you."

The Bug Detector was the unofficial name we gave to the little device one of our members had constructed to make sure rooms and buildings were clean of the cops. Viper was gorgeous in a predatory sort of way and she could strike as fast as the reptile for which she was named.

134

She also was smart, sharp, and vigilant. She had items even Neo didn't know about, and her cabin was the only one Neo couldn't see into.

"Why would I take that with me? For the warehouse?"

"No. For Oriana's place."

Michael's statement made my stomach lurch and my blood go cold. "You think someone's spyin' on her?"

I could almost hear him shake his head. "I dunno. But my gut says she might not have been as cut off from the FBI as she thought."

Anger surged. No one should've been surveilling her but me, and not even I would do shit like that. "She's gonna be pissed about that and think we knew before we go to her place."

"Guess you're just gonna have to actually talk to her, then, mate. Text me when you get to Fort Collins."

He clicked off with that smug voice that made me want to thump him good the next time I saw him. As it was, I hated to admit he was right and there was nothing I could do about that, either. Instead I had to wait for my laundry to finish and that gave me plenty of time to decide what I'd try to say to Oriana on the way to Fort Collins.

Yeah, this is gonna suck.

****

Scott

I climbed into the cab of our van, the delivery kind seen more often in Europe than the U.S., and closed the door behind me. I didn't want to look at the passenger side where Arctic cold seeped from the person seated there. Oriana sat, buckled in, with her arms crossed over her chest and her face set. She stared out the window and refused to turn her head, for which I counted my blessings. She'd freeze my balls off with her anger.

I started the van and put it in gear, trying not to get frostbite in my right elbow. I thanked my lucky stars she wasn't Viper or Calhoun. Both those women did vicious and permanent damage to those who pissed them off, though I wouldn't put it past Numbers to make someone's life financial hell. *Who am I kidding? It's my life she's gonna fuck up.*

I turned onto the main road and headed for Fort Collins in a silence reserved for desert wastelands and Arctic tundra. Somewhere in my head I could hear the sound of a lonely guitar and the scream of a hunting Red Tail Hawk. This was the essence of No Man's Land and I was stuck behind the wheel of it.

"Why am I here?" Oriana's voice cracked like a whip and I jumped.

"Uh, you're comin' with me to Fort Collins." Why did she think she was here?

"I know that. The question is why. Loki made it clear I had to stay at the compound." If her look had death-ray capabilities, I would've been half-way to hell by now.

"Yeah, I know. I was there." I winced and bit my bottom lip as soon as the words left my mouth. *So you're goin' for full asshole today, are you, Scott?* "I mean, I know he said that, but I have to run down to one of our warehouses in Fort Collins and I found out it's near your apartment. Michael thought we could stop and get some of your things to make your cabin feel like home."

"My apartment is home, not the compound. I did what I said I would and y'all are liars and cheats." She went back to staring out the window. "I was just stupid enough to believe otherwise. Not the first time I was wrong about men having integrity."

I gritted my teeth at the venom in her voice. It didn't help she was right. At least about Loki. I thought I had integrity, but evidently not enough to make Loki's about-face clear from the get-go.

"I'm not a liar, but I am sorry I didn't speak up about the likelihood of you leaving after you fulfilled your contract." I tried to keep my voice even despite the anger at her words. She was right to be angry and I was a jackass, but it didn't make it easy to admit. "I should've said something. I should've warned you what he's like. But I didn't think it would matter."

"You didn't think it would *matter*?" She widened her eyes as her lips pulled back from her teeth. "I made it clear how important my independence was to me. I made the terms of the contract clear as I could. Why wouldn't it matter?"

"Because I hoped I could convince you to stay on your own."

"How were you planning to do that?"

"I, uh. Well, I..." My ability to talk hopped a freight train to nowhere and left me hanging.

How was I supposed to tell this woman that I wanted her without sounding like a complete and utter moron? Oriana represented everything I desired in a woman. She was smart, intuitive, funny, kinky, bold, inquisitive, sexy, and beautiful, and I wanted to be with her for a long time. I hoped to give her my patch of ownership and call her mine.

But I knew deep down that she wasn't a person to be owned, even if that's not what the patch would mean to me. To her, she'd see "Property of Scott" as being an object, a possession, rather than as my partner and confidante. But I didn't want anyone messing with her, and wearing my patch would save a lot of headaches.

"Whatever. Let's just get this shit over with."

Michael's voice echoed in my head: *Begin with "I'm sorry." Continue with "Please forgive me." And possibly add, "What can I do to make it up to you?"* I'd accomplished the first part, I just had to grow a pair to continue.

"I was hoping to convince you to go out with me long

term, then you having to stay wouldn't matter so much because you already would." There, I'd said it. Hopefully I wouldn't get my head bitten off.

"You know I could've gone out with you long term without living in the compound, don't you? It's called having a girlfriend offsite. If you'd just made a little effort, we could've had a good relationship." She scowled. "I wouldn't have gone anywhere. Fort Collins isn't that far from the compound, you know."

"I know, but I just wanted you to stay." Damn, I sounded like a whiney pansy-ass.

"Why didn't you say anything? I can't read your mind. Cocky bikers are incomprehensible to me."

"I didn't have time. You were focused on finding the embezzler and I didn't want to push you into anything scary. I know what Hopkins did and I didn't want to be that guy, the one who doesn't listen to you or think about what you needed." I shrugged as we drove into the residential areas outside of Fort Collins. "I thought I'd court you, y'know? I wanted to get to know you and make you like me without being too aggressive. And I, I dunno, didn't think you'd give me that chance if you weren't there where I could see you at meals and hang out with you."

I had no idea where this touchy-feely shit was coming from, but all of it was true. I meant every word, and it felt like someone had scraped my heart raw. I wouldn't have admitted it to any of the other women I'd been with over the years, but I couldn't stop myself from telling Oriana.

I shot a look at her as we turned into the area of her apartment complex and she blinked back at me, her eyes wide. *Glory, I hope that's not a bad thing and she's not trying to find a way to let me down easy.*

"I—hmm. How long have you felt this way?"

I shrugged again and pulled the van up to the curb in front of her apartment building. "Pretty much since you dictated the terms of your contract to Loki. Damn, you were sexy, bold, and beautiful, and you weren't gonna take anyone's shit. That lit my fire right there." I put the van in park and set the break, before turning off the engine.

Come on, you wuss. Tell her the rest.

I raised my gaze to meet hers and took a deep breath. "I really like you, Oriana. Actually, it's more than that, but the word "love" makes me nervous because I've never loved anyone before. Not really. I've wanted to ask you to wear my patch lots of times, but I know how you feel about being someone's property, and I couldn't do that to you." I rubbed the back of my neck. "But I want more than just a romp in the sheets. Hell, I liked getting my ass handed to me in pool by you. And I want more of that."

"You liked that I beat the pants off you, literally?" She tilted her had and I hoped the smirk was ready to come out.

"Hell yeah. I liked playing and I liked what came after." I tried my own grin. "To be honest, I like a lot of things with you. I'm sorry Loki pulled a fast one. I suspected he'd do something, but I didn't know exactly what. But I want to make it better for you, as much as I can, because bein' without you fucking sucks."

She grimaced and looked out her window at the apartment building. "Yeah, I haven't enjoyed being alone either." She turned back to me. "I'm sorry I didn't give you a chance to explain your side of things. I was just so mad that I'd believed Loki would honor the contract that I blamed you for something I should've known."

She shook her head and rubbed her fingers over the hem of her shirt. "I don't like being trapped or tricked, and Loki did both. I should've seen it coming. Actually, I did. I told Mel I wouldn't go up to the compound with her because you can always check out but you can never leave."

I nodded slowly. "The Hotel California reference."

"Yeah. And now I essentially know too much. Loki can't afford for me to leave." She stared at her apartment.

139

"It's only been a week since I left, but it feels like a lifetime."

"It wasn't all bad, was it?" Glory, I wouldn't handle it well if she was miserable with me.

"No. And according to the contract, I'm to be treated as a full member of the club, or he has to let me leave." I winced, but she waved it away. "Oh, I know. That's probably voided because the project he had me working on is over. But I think I've earned my place without being someone's property." She gave me a half-smile. "What about giving you my patch?"

"What?" I must've blinked owlishly because she laughed.

"Sure. You could be the Property of Numbers. You'd be the Numbers' Man."

She grinned while I gaped like a fish. I'd never considered belonging to anyone, and despite the connotations of ownership, the idea warmed my chest unlike anything before.

I want to belong to her.

The thought slammed into me and stunned me. I must've looked like a deer in headlights because she patted my arm.

"Don't worry. I was just kidding—"

"I'll wear it."

"What?" It was her turn to blink.

"I'd wear it in a heartbeat. I'd wear your property patch. I'd add it to my cut."

"You would? Why?" She shot me perplexed look.

"Because I'd be fuckin' proud to belong to you."

CHAPTER THIRTEEN

Oriana

I think I stopped breathing for a minute in the cab of the van. Scott had just told me he'd wear *my* property patch. I wasn't a biker. Hell, I'd never ridden on a motorcycle and didn't plan to start. And I was a frickin' prisoner of the club. But he'd wear my patch.

"You're serious."

"Yeah." He looked relaxed and serene like when I arrived at the compound, totally sure of himself. "Yeah, belonging to you would rock my world."

My brain fizzled to a stop. I'd never heard of a biker belonging to a woman, it was always the other way around. I stared at him, trying to figure out where the break in translation had occurred and I had to rewind the conversation a little to start again.

"I think I've missed something. What does wearing a patch really mean to you?"

"It means you're my partner, someone I share secrets and dreams with, and you know, sex and stuff." Scott frowned as he tried to find words to explain. "The property patch isn't really an ownership thing for me, but it does save time with the other men trying to hit on you when you're already taken."

I rolled my eyes. "That means they still fear reprisals from you more than respecting me for telling them no."

He grimaced and nodded. "Yeah, this world is fucked up like that. But what does it matter what other people think when you and I know the truth?"

"I wish it was that easy, Scott. But I've learned otherwise. I knew the truth about what happened to me at the FBI, and I lost my job because of what other people thought." I waved the depressing thoughts away. "That part doesn't matter, and you wearing my property patch won't affect your job, or mine, but the experience is pretty bitter."

"Oh, yeah, I guess I hadn't thought of that." He sighed. "Here's the thing. You said no one believed you, that they believed the lie. But if our definition of the property patch is shared by me and you, that's two against the others, and they can go fuck themselves."

He met my gaze with an earnestness and vulnerability I'd never seen in him before.

"I don't want to be with anyone else, Numbers. When Melrose brought you to the compound, I thought you were just another biker groupie. When I realized you really didn't want to be there, I started to pay attention." He grimaced. "Yeah, I'm a jackass, I know. But you were more than just a honey looking for some biker cock and it made me take notice. Hanging out with you and having you around this past week has been good. Better than good. The best week in a long fuckin' time. But it made me realize I don't want you to leave. I wanna see you every day and talk about numbers or pool or whatever. I want to belong to you. Hell, I'm pretty sure I do already. And I'm pretty sure you belong with me. So whadya say?"

While it wasn't the most elegant of declarations, it still warmed my heart and made my world a little brighter.

"Would you really wear a patch on your cut that says Property of Numbers?"

"Hell yeah." He reached out and grasped my hand. "I know Loki's deal with you sucks, that he weaseled his way into something he shouldn't. But I'd wear your patch and lose at pool every chance I get if you'd stay and be my woman."

I glanced down at his hands wrapped around mine and let that idea roll around in my head. I'd disdained Mel for going out with a biker because their relationship always seemed to suck. I wasn't wrong about them, but I didn't think my relationship with Scott would be the same. For all his rough edges, I liked him. He was honorable and kind and generous in his own way. And he'd definitely make my forced residence in the Concrete Angels much better.

"Okay, Scott. It's a deal. So help me load up my shit and we'll take it back to the compound."

"Fuck yeah!" He roared the phrase as he pulled me close for a hard kiss. "Best fuckin' news I've heard in weeks. Let's get your shit."

I laughed as he released me and we got out of the van. My heart felt lighter, too, and I shook my head at the craziness of life. Falling for a rough biker like Scott seemed way outside my purview, but now that I had, I couldn't imagine my life without him in it. I pulled my keys out of my purse as we headed for the door, him jogging up the stairs with a bounce in his step.

"Do you have boxes?" He waited for me to put the key in door.

I shook my head. "I have plastic totes instead. Easier to pack up and move if I had to."

Regret washed over his face. "I guess that's good, right?"

I shrugged. "Yeah, it'll make this move easier."

I started to push the door open, but he stopped me. "Hold on just a second." He dug something out of his pocket that looked like a thick magic wand. It had a power button on the handle and two little lightbulbs on the blunt end.

"What's that?"

"Bug and camera detector. Viper made it. Works great." He waved it at the front room of my apartment. "We'll check it over to make sure there aren't any."

"You think someone's bugged my apartment?" The idea repulsed and infuriated me. What the fuck?

"No, I'm makin' sure it's not."

But we weren't that lucky. To my horror, we found a camera in my kitchen and another in my bedroom, and audio bugs in both, plus the living room. Thank goodness I hadn't had any sexual partners to my place since I'd moved there.

"Damn, Numbers, someone's keepin' tabs on you." Scott collected the little surveillance devices and threw them into one of my old sunglasses cases, zipping it shut. "I'm gonna take these out to the van."

I wanted to smash the offending little things, but he whisked them away before I could say anything. *The less I say the better, I guess.* Who would be targeting me for surveillance? I couldn't imagine the FBI wanted to know where I was after I'd left them. Yeah, I'd signed a nondisclosure agreement for the top secret stuff I'd worked on, but I didn't think they'd care beyond that. I wasn't a field agent so I didn't know what kind of equipment they used, but I knew they had the capability.

I scowled and headed for my closets, a shiver ripping through me. My own home, my place of sanctuary, wasn't safe. Whoever was watching and listening had violated it. At the moment, my cabin at the Concrete Angels' compound sounded a helluva lot better. I knew that wasn't bugged. I'd checked regularly.

I should've checked here, too.

I threw my clothes into my suitcases and my few

knickknacks into my totes, fury growing by the minute. Scott came back in and helped me clear out most of the bedroom and master bath, but as I tore at the bed, he caught my hands.

"Whoa, wait, hold on there." He met my furious gaze and tilted his head. "What's wrong?"

"What's wrong? Someone fucking bugged my home and watched me. What do you think is wrong?"

"But we found them, and they haven't had anything to watch for over a week, right?" He turned me until I faced him. "I have them in a dark, quiet spot until we get back to the compound. I bet Neo can backtrack and find out where they're sending the information. Then we can find out who it was."

"You know the FBI has gear like that."

He nodded. "The NSA, too. Most of the federal alphabet agencies do. But right now, I'm not worried about them."

I raised an eyebrow. "You're not?"

"Nope. I'm more concerned with making you feel good."

I blinked. "What?"

He crowded me back toward the bed with a sexy, predatory look. If it had been anyone else, I'd have panicked. But I knew I was safe with Scott, even when my knees hit the end of the bed.

"Before we strip the bed, I think we should put it to good use. Nobody's around, no one can hear us who knows us, and it's been too long since I've made you feel good. So whadaya say?"

It took me a few moments to understand what he proposed, but when it became clear, I expected panic and an extreme need to get away. But the only emotions I felt were arousal and need and lust. Apparently, my subconscious mind trusted Scott.

"You want to make love to me?"

"I want to make love *with* you. It ain't fun for me if you're not having fun."

I grimaced. "You know what I mean."

"I do, but I want it clear that while I might like hot, rough sex, I don't do it without consent." He ran his hands up my arms until he cupped my face. "Your pleasure is more important to me than blowing my wad. I can do that anytime. So how 'bout I feast on that pussy of yours and make you come hard?"

"Okay." It was an inane answer, but I didn't see the need to argue. I'd experienced his cunnilingus before and there was no way in hell I'd say no to it now.

"Hell yeah. Let me take care of you, Oriana." He knelt at my feet with a hungry grin. "Have I told you I love it when you wear these short pants? They're fuckin' sexy on your ass and legs."

He peeled off my capris in a slow reveal that made me shiver. I thanked my lucky stars they had a stretchy waist. Not only did they hug my hips in an elegant curve, but they came off in a sexy slide without resistance.

"Oh, fuck yeah, you wore satin and lace."

They were an old pair of panties I'd found in the clearance bin at that fancy underwear shop at the mall and I'd bought them to make myself feel sexy. I'd never expected someone would care if I wore them, but Scott hummed and growled as he slid his fingers over their surface. The front had red satin with black lace trim and little plastic rhinestones. The butt panel, however, was all black lace.

Scott ran his hands over the lace and moaned. "Fuck me, those are the sexiest panties I've ever seen."

I raised my eyebrows. "They are?"

"Oh yeah. They show off your pretty pussy and the crack of your ass even while you're "covered." It's erotic as hell." He skimmed his fingers under the lace on my ass and squeezed. "It covers you without hiding anything."

I rested my hands on his shoulders as he met my gaze, his fingers still caressing my butt. "Do you like what you see?"

"Hell yeah." He leaned forward and kissed my satin-covered mound. "I also like what I smell."

I blinked. "You can smell me?"

"Yup, and it's like Palisade Peaches and cream." He inhaled and closed his eyes. "Damn, so sweet and tasty. I can't wait to lick your pussy again."

I pushed back from him and scrambled onto the bed. "You want to taste it? Bring it on. I've missed your tongue." I had no idea where the boldness came from, but I liked watching Scott's eyes flare with arousal when I gave it to him.

He growled, I kid you not, and whipped his cut and T-shirt over his head. I didn't have much time to admire the heavily muscled chest with dark hair arrowing down his abs to his jeans. The image stayed in my mind as he kicked off his boots and crawled onto the bed to push his shoulders between my knees.

"Let's peel these sexy panties off you and save them. I'm wanna see them on you again." He pulled the elastic off my hips and down my legs then brought the scrap of satin and lace to his nose. "Damn, those smell good. I'll put them in my pocket for safe-keeping."

He stuffed the cloth in to his back pocket and I laughed.

"You're gonna let me put those back on when we're done, right?"

He winked. "We'll see. Now, lie back and let me get to work."

I smirked. "What, no foreplay and teasing?"

"No time for that, darlin'. We gotta get you packed up and the warehouse cleared out before the FBI comes lookin'. I don't want them anywhere near my woman."

"I'm your woman now, am I?"

He raised his head to meet my gaze without his usual smirk. "Yeah, Oriana. You're mine, as much as I'm yours. No ifs, ands, or buts."

I believed him. It wasn't logical, but this cocky biker had won my heart by backing me up, sticking with me, and never giving up on me. Most guys had walked away when I freaked out, but Scott didn't seem to have "quit" in his vocabulary.

"Okay." There was that lame word again, but I'd gotten so choked up, it was the best I could manage.

He grinned and squeezed my hips before he dipped his head and licked my slit. My eyes rolled back in my head at the hot ticklish sensations he delivered. He moaned into my sensitive flesh and I answered him with my own. I'd never met a man so skilled with his tongue and I wasn't letting him go.

Scott wrapped his arms around my thighs and used his fingers to peel apart my nether lips. Hot, wet pleasure pulsed through me as he slid his tongue between my folds and rubbed my clit. I'd given myself pleasure before, but nothing came close to Scott sucking on my clit. He hummed and the vibration sparked my arousal.

In addition to the building orgasm, a new feeling grew in my chest. Something warmer and fuller than lust, more potent than desire. It had shades of trust and awareness as well as a splash of hope and acceptance.

Is this what love feels like? I'd read about it in romance novels. I'd seen examples in movies and TV shows. But I hadn't experienced it from another person outside of family, and even theirs had been conditional.

My heart filled with this feeling as Scott built up my pleasure with his clever tongue. He licked my slit as he pressed one of my legs to the bed. He skimmed his hand along my inner thigh, splintering my thoughts with zings of pleasure.

"Oh, glory, Scott. I love it when you do this."

He hummed his approval and worked a finger into my pussy, flicking my clit with his tongue. I whimpered and tightened my hands in the sheets. He thrust his hand slowly, scraping against my g-spot with inexorable pressure. I wriggled my hips, trying to get closer to his finger, but he pulled it away and licked my folds.

I moaned and rocked my hips, harder, and he pulled his head away. "What do you want, Oriana?"

"More, harder."

"More like this?" He inserted a second finger, stretching my tight sheath.

"Yes, oh, glory, yes." I tried to match his rhythm, but I wanted faster and he kept it steady. "Please, Scott. I need faster."

He chuckled. "I'll give it to you, but I want you to come hard, and the steady rhythm will make it last longer."

I couldn't argue with that, but the delicious tickling of his tongue on my nether lips and clit revved me up until I wanted more. He thrust his fingers deep into my pussy, curling them just enough to scrape my g-spot. Each time made me gasp and arch into his touch.

I want this all the time.

The thought pushed through the building orgasm, propelling me deeper into the surging pleasure. When Scott sucked hard on my clit, thrusting his hand at the same time, I was a goner. My arousal broke over me in shooting wave, flooding my awareness with ecstasy and a need for more. More pleasure, more intimacy, more Scott.

I'd never been sexually aggressive, even before my rape, but this orgasm ignited a need to roll him over and ride him hard. I wanted to see him go all soft and boneless with pleasure himself.

Scott hummed his approval of my release, lapping it up as if he couldn't get enough. I lay there and panted as he lifted his head away, wiping his mouth. A satisfied smirk curled his lips as he crawled up the bed to lie beside me.

That's my cocky biker.

But I wasn't going to lie around. He had a lovely stiff shaft that needed tending and I wanted its attention. I rolled over on top of him, pressing his cock between my breasts as I licked my lips. His eyes widened and the smirk faded as I wriggled between his legs.

"That was wonderful and I like my pussy licked. But now I need your hard cock. You got a condom on you?"

"Fuck yeah." His voice came out like he'd chewed a mouthful of gravel. "In the back pocket of my jeans."

I slid backward off the bed, my pussy aching for more, and he growled as my breasts dragged against his shaft. I laughed but I wasn't interested in taking any more time than he wanted to wait. My hot lover watched me with his desire flaring in his eyes as I sauntered to his jeans, bent over with my ass facing him, and pulled the condom packets from the pocket. *The man comes prepared.* He'd brought three condoms and I liked his Boy Scout style.

I stood up, waving the packets. "Optimistic, aren't you?"

"Hell yeah. I didn't want to be unprepared if you gave me the chance." He grinned.

I tore one off the strip and opened it as I returned to the bed. "I like a man who knows what he wants and has the equipment ready." I grasped his cock and massaged it with my hand before I rolled the condom on. "And your equipment is just the kind I like." I swung my leg over his hips, gazing down at him for a few moments.

His beauty took my breath away. The heavy slabs of muscle on his chest gave way to his cobbled abs, and the "happy trail" leading straight to his groin. I loved the strength in his neck and shoulders, and the smoky arousal in his green eyes. The trimmed beard and short hair on his head framed a face as rugged as it was beautiful, and I reached out to run my hand down his bearded cheek.

"I'm going to ride you, Scott, enjoying your rigid cock

in my pussy until I can't hold back anymore." His gaze intensified on me with my words. "I'm going to enjoy these hard muscles between my legs like I did your bearded face on my pussy. I want you to fuck me slow and deep because I want to remember this when the panic gets to me. I want to overwrite those old memories with new ones."

"Then let me be your editor and we'll revise your sexy story." He grasped my hips as I pointed his cock toward my pussy. "I want to be the only one you remember."

I wanted that, too. I sank down on his dick and we both moaned as I seated him all the way to his balls. I met his fiery green gaze and liked the intensity I could read in his expression.

"Holy shit, you're tight, Oriana."

I moaned. "That's a good thing, right?"

"Fuck yeah, it's good. It's gonna be even better when you move. Fuck me slow and deep, darlin'."

His words turned me on, but the pleasurable friction between my legs pushed my arousal higher as I rose up and sank back down. He rocked his hips, matching my rhythm, and met my gaze with an anticipatory smile.

"Good glory, ride me, Oriana. Fuck, that's so sexy."

I braced my hands on his hard chest, enjoying the motion of his muscles under them. I loved the wet sounds of me sliding off him and the delicious thumps when we came together. I loved the contrast of his inked skin along my thigh, the dark lines flexing with his motions.

Glory, that's sexy.

Sweat showed at his temples, wetting the dark hair, and his nipples hardened to sharp little points under my hands. I wanted to lean down to lick them, but I wasn't that flexible and I didn't want to lose connection with his thick cock.

"Oh glory, Scott. It feels so good. I love fucking your cock." I meant every word as my arousal built with each thrust and retreat.

True to his word, he kept the rhythm deep and slow and I couldn't fight my orgasm surging through me. It started like a little puddle of nectar at the back of my mind, burbling with each slide of his dick against my vagina's walls. But he arched his back and the head of his cock scraped over my g-spot, electrifying my release.

I wailed my delight as it surged through me, making me rock harder against his hard shaft. His cock hardened even more and his own shout of pleasure shook the walls as he hit his release. Hot spurts of cum filled my pussy and my orgasm continued until I collapsed on him, panting hard.

"I love you, Oriana." Scott gasped the statement into my hair as I rose and fell on his chest.

"What did you say?" I used one hand to lever myself up so I could see his face, my heart pounding.

"I said I love you." He stared at me with wonder, and I suspected my expression matched his. "I love you and want to be your man forever. Stay with me in the Concrete Angels. Not because Loki had you sign a contract, but because you're my woman and my lover. Please."

It was the please that got me. Scott didn't ask for things from anyone. Mostly that was because he was an arrogant jackass and had the confidence no one could shake. But having him ask me to stay, putting his heart and vulnerability into his words, won me over faster than anything else could have.

I tilted my head as excitement surged. "Will I still get my own space to work? Will I still get paid for the work I've done or will do?"

"Yeah. We'll work out a new contract." His seafoam green eyes filled with new emotion, something I hadn't seen there when I first met him. Hope.

I wiggled my hips and clenched my inner muscles around his softening shaft, making him moan. "And will you be my exclusive fuck-buddy and lover?"

A smirk curled his lips. "Hell yeah."

I laughed. "All right, you got yourself a deal." Then I leaned forward and kissed the living daylights out of him.

CHAPTER FOURTEEN

Scott

"I think that's the last of it."

I took the box of books from Oriana and loaded it into the van as she worked the key to her apartment off the keyring. I damn near skipped to the front of the van. Hell, I felt so fuckin' good, I could've done cartwheels and handstands. Oriana had accepted my declaration of love and said she wanted to stay in the Concrete Angels. *With me.* Aw yeah, I done scored better than I ever had before.

She locked the door of the apartment and joined me in the cab of the van. I could barely sit still as pleasure and excitement ran through me at her presence. Yeah, we'd fucked hard in the apartment, probably embarrassed the hell out of the neighbors, but the idea of having more sex with Oriana lit my fire, big time. I wouldn't push her, I'd just let it flow.

"I'm going to drop this off." She waved the key at me as we drove closer to the rental office. "Then I'm ready to leave."

"Sounds good. I'll be here. Gonna check in with the

crew cleaning up today." The bugs in the zipped up sunglasses case might be muffled, but not disabled.

I picked up the case and got out of the van as Oriana headed for the office. I didn't know who was listening in, but I'd rather our news didn't get broadcasted to whoever it was. *Probably the FBI.* Maybe, but it could be someone else, like her former supervisor.

I opened the back doors of the van and shoved the sunglasses case into a suitcase full of Oriana's clothes. It would be muffled enough for us to get them to Neo and still make plans.

I closed the door and dialed Michael's number as I walked back to the driver's side door.

"Michael here."

"Hey, Schnoz, how's it hanging?"

"Long, and heavy, and always to the right." The amusement in my best buddy's voice made me grin. "How'd it go with Oriana? Did she get her things?"

"Yeah, got her all packed up and moved out."

"What?" Michael barked it into the phone. "You weren't supposed to move her now. You were supposed to give her time, Scott."

"Hey, I didn't make this decision. It was all her." I waved at the building even though he couldn't see it. "How's it goin' at the warehouse on Converse?"

"Attila says they have a 'wee bit' left to do, but you know how it is with him. A 'wee bit' could be loading the last vehicle or half the building is left on the floor." I could hear Michael roll his eyes. "In any case, can you swing by on your way back to the compound to see how it's going?"

"Yeah, we'll do that." I nodded as Oriana came back out of the office. "Hey, do me a favor and let Neo and Viper know we're bringing in some bugs and cameras. They were all over Oriana's apartment. Someone wanted to know what she was doing and who she was with. I want to know where the feeds were going and how long they've been in place."

"Shit, someone was watching and listening?"

"Yeah, and if I had to guess, I'd say it was the FBI given the equipment I found. This wasn't run-of-the-mill stuff, Schnoz, it's high quality, damn-near military grade. Sneaky shit. If I didn't have Viper's doodad, we wouldn't have known." I rubbed the back of my neck. "I gotta go, but tell Viper thanks and Neo that we'll have some snooping to do. I wanna know who's keeping tabs on Numbers."

"Right. See you when you get back here."

"Yeah. Later." I hung up and looked at Oriana as she climbed into the van. "We all good?"

She nodded. "They won't give me my deposit back, but then I didn't spend much time cleaning. Not sure where to forward my mail to, though."

"We'll get you a PO box in Skin Gulch." I turned on the van and threw it in drive. "We gotta stop by the…" I shot a look back at her things riding in the van. "Storage unit to check on the crew. You okay with that?"

Oriana narrowed her eyes. "Storage unit?"

"Yeah, you know, the other place we had to go down here in Fort Collins." I hoped she wouldn't need more of an explanation. I didn't know how sensitive the listening devices that we'd pulled out of her place were. "Schnoz asked me to drop by to see how it was going."

"Oh. Oh! Yeah, I remember now." She nodded. "That's fine." She grasped her phone and started texting someone. I tried not to be jealous as I eased into traffic. *You can't be her only contact, jackass.* But the Neanderthal in me wanted to be. Oh yeah, I was a Grade A idiot.

I was still stewing when we stopped at a light and I glanced over at her. She held up her phone so I could read the text and I gave myself a mental head slap. The words on the screen read:

SOMEONE'S LISTENING, RIGHT? THAT'S WHY

WE'RE NOT TALKING ABOUT THE WAREHOUSE.
Relief crashed through me that she wasn't texting
anyone and I still gave myself another mental head slap. *I
gotta get this Neanderthal under control.* I nodded to her
text.

She took the phone back and added something.
WHY ARE WE KEEPING THE DAMN THINGS IF
THEY'RE STILL WORKING?

"Can I have the phone?" I held my hand out for it as
we headed toward the industrial side of town. She set it in
my palm. "Thanks."

I kept my eyes on the road, aware that I shouldn't be
texting while driving, but we were on a straight-away and
no cops were around. I typed out my message and handed
the phone back to her just in time to make the turn onto
Converse.

NEO CAN TRACE SIGNALS BACK TO SOURCE.
FIND OUT WHO'S LISTENING TO YOU AND TRACK
THEM DOWN.

She nodded slowly as she typed again.
DO YOU THINK IT'S THE FBI?

I shrugged when I saw the screen and turned on the
radio. When Barry Manilow belted out a sappy love song I
jumped and yanked the dial to something else. I managed
to find Britney Spears, Justin Bieber, and Taylor Swift in
quick succession, and glanced at Oriana in horror.

She laughed and set it to a station playing Def Leppard
and I shuddered in relief.

"Good glory, I didn't think we'd survive." I shot her a
relieved look as I parked the van at the end of the
warehouse, far enough that the bugs wouldn't pick up on
any conversations inside.

"Who used the van last?" She laughed as she got out.

"I dunno, but they gotta get over their Manilow fetish."
I shook my head. "I'll be bringing it up at the next club
meeting for sure." I locked the van and we headed into the

warehouse where two larger vans sat almost full of cargo.

"Hey Attila, how's it goin'?" I called out as soon as I saw the big Scot. He had bright green eyes and long curly hair with two or three braids in it. We'd learned not to tease him about the hair when he'd put one of the Scooters through a wall for harassing him about it.

"Hey, Scott, comin' to check up on me, are ye?" Attila grasped my forearm and slapped my shoulder with his free hand. "As ye can see, we got it all done wi'out ye."

I nodded as I watched the Scooters and some of the other members hosing the place down and sweeping out the excess water.

"Schnoz sent me since I was in the area. Just making sure you didn't need any extra help. Looks like things are set."

"Aye, there'll be nothin' left for those bastards to find. Pain in the arse, it is, but worth the looks on their poxy faces." Attila shot a look at Oriana and frowned. "Wait, isn't she one o' them? What the fook is she doin' here?"

Oriana straightened her back, but clamped her lips together and I scowled back at him.

"No, you jackass, she's not one of them. She works for us now, and she sure as hell doesn't report to them. And you better get used to her being around."

"Oh yeah, why's that?" Attila raised an eyebrow.

"Because she'll be wearin' my patch and takin' care of your paychecks."

Attila's jaw dropped and he shot a look at Oriana before swinging back to me. "Are ye fookin' out of yer mind? Why would ye trust her? She's a Fed, for glory's sake."

"She's *not* a Fed, she's part of the club, and she knows where all the money is. She signed in blood with Loki."

Attila's thick eyebrows went up and his chin lifted as he scratched his beard in consideration. "Did ye really sign a blood contract with Loki, lassie?"

Oriana grimaced and nodded. "Yeah."

"Och, dinna ye know better than to do that?" Attila shook his head. "I hope you got somethin' worthwhile outta it."

She tilted her head and slanted a look toward me. "I think I did, but it's early yet. I'll let you know in a few days."

He threw back his head and laughed. "Aye, that's the spirit. I like ye, lassie. Have ye got a name?"

Now she laughed. "Several, but you can call me…" She shot me a considering look. "Numbers."

I don't know why my chest puffed out and I stood a little straighter, but it was hard to keep the smirk off my face when Attila narrowed his eyes at me.

"Is that because you look at all the wee numbers we bring in?"

"Maybe it's me being an ignorant American, but I thought 'wee' means 'small or little', and I've seen your income streams. There's nothing small or little about them."

Attila grinned. "Och, aye, I know it. But we doona want to give the IRS any clue to that, now do we?" He winked.

Oriana shook her head with a chuckle. "Right."

"So are you finished with the packing up? I gotta get Numbers back to the clubhouse so she can get settled."

"Aye, it's done. The Scooters are washin' the place down and we'll be out of here in a trice."

"Good. I'll text Schnoz and we'll be ready for when the Feds show up." I needed to get Oriana away from the handsome Scot. I knew how women fawned over his brogue and his rugged good looks. I'd seen too many fall for his charms.

"Good. And Numbers, if ye get tired of Scott's half-assed attempts to woo ye, my cabin's number fourteen." Attila winked again.

My inner Neanderthal stood up and threatened to beat his chest again as a growl rumbled in my throat. I swallowed against the sound, but Oriana heard it and patted my arm.

"Come on. Take me home. I want to find out who bugged my place."

My anger returned, but it shifted toward the unknown watchers. "Yeah, and I don't want those bugs picking up things they shouldn't." I met Attila's gaze. "If you don't need any help, we'll just head back up to the compound."

"No, we're all good here. See you at the clubhouse." He waved and winked at Numbers but she turned with me without a look back. *Eat your heart out, you Scottish bastard.*

We climbed back into the van and chatted about mundane things like the latest movies coming out and which fast food was the best. I maintained you couldn't beat a cheesey pizza with sausage and onions, while she insisted the best food in the world was Mongolian grill where you picked the things you wanted while someone else cooked it.

The conversation kept going until we drove in the gates of the compound. I parked the van in front of her cabin to make the unloading go easier. Dollhouse, Karma, and Michael helped unload and haul her totes into the cabin while I took the sunglasses case into the clubhouse and straight to Neo's lair.

"Took you long enough." He looked up from his monitors. "Are those what I think they are?"

I wanted to be snarky, but I didn't want to give the potential listeners anything to go on. "Yup."

"I'll take them and see what I can find out."

"Thanks." I grabbed a sticky note and wrote down a few words: *FBI? Someone else? How long?*

I handed him the paper and raised my eyebrows.

"Yeah, I'll check on all that."

"Good. Catch you later."

I headed back out to help Oriana move in and take care of the van. The idea that someone had been watching and listening to her in her own home infuriated me. She'd been through enough and I'd be damned before I let it continue.

Satisfaction settled into my gut as I joined the people unloading the van. We'd cleared out the compound and the warehouses of contraband, I'd convinced Oriana to live at the compound permanently, and we'd fucked like rabbits. All in all, a damn good day.

CHAPTER FIFTEEN

Oriana

Despite the Concrete Angels' sense of urgency, the FBI didn't raid the compound until two days later. I'd always thought shit happened on random Tuesdays, and the FBI didn't disappoint. Fortunately, I'd recovered my personal Glock 43 when we packed up my apartment and I maintained both my weapon and my gun license. I hadn't carried in months, but I felt safer with it in my cabin and control.

When the FBI showed up at the compound conducting a raid and waving a warrant, the guy they called the Friar let them in with a psychotic grin and a maniacal look in his eyes. People dressed in blue jackets with FBI in bright yellow lettering swarmed into the compound. Those of us sitting outside enjoying the cool breeze didn't even do more than look up. I'd just reached the good part of a romantic suspense novel. There was no way I'd put it down for an FBI raid. It was rather fun to see them flustered with our lack of concern.

The FBI isn't used to being ignored.

Scott walked out of the clubhouse carrying a plastic basket of laundry on his hip like a washer woman, his eyebrows up. Dollhouse leaned against the Ponderosa, cleaning her fingernails with a pocket knife. Most of the Scooters lounging around got to their feet, their faces angry. But Michael, Loki, Attila and a new man I hadn't seen before came out of the clubhouse with mild curiosity on their faces.

"What can we do for you gentlemen and ladies?" Loki waved to all the FBI agents swarming around the yard.

"I'm Agent In Charge Cisneros and we've got a warrant to search the place for drugs and weapons." The hard-eyed man shook the warrant at Loki. "You need to open everything up."

Loki tilted his head. "What makes you think there's anything to find here, Agent? We're a motorcycle club, and unlike those TV shows and movies you must love to watch, we aren't into weapons or drugs, *ja*?" He swung his gaze to me but kept going until he stopped on someone a few doors down. I followed his line of sight to catch Roy cross his arms over his chest.

Oh ho, Loki's onto you, bad boy, and you know it.

I had to give Roy credit. He didn't flinch. I would've been whimpering and sweating if Loki looked at me that way.

"We'll see about that, won't we?" The agent in charge waved the warrant again.

"Let me see that." A woman I'd never seen before strode up to take the warrant out of the belligerent agent's hand.

"And who are you?"

"Abigail Charles, attorney for the Concrete Angels." She didn't bother to look up at the agent as she scanned the document.

"All right, start checking all the buildings."

"Hold it." Abigail's voice cracked like a whip and all

the agents froze. "It says here you only have permission to search the club's community buildings such as the barn, sheds, garage, and clubhouse. You cannot search the personal residences of the members, including the barracks."

The agents who'd been headed toward me and my cabin paused and looked back at the AIC. Abigail held out the paper with one hand and pushed up her wire-rimmed glasses with the other. The AIC snatched the paper with a scowl and reread it, and I bit my lips to keep from laughing. I hadn't been on any field assignments when I worked for the FBI, but I could see his frustration at the limitations on the warrant.

"Fuck." He didn't say it loud, but I could hear it clearly enough. "She's right. Just the community buildings only."

"What the fuck?"

Everything inside of me froze in panic and my hands shook on the paperback. I knew that voice. I'd heard it raised in anger and laughing with colleagues in the break room. I'd heard it giving orders. And I'd heard it hoarse with sexual arousal and inexorable demand.

I raised my gaze from the fluttering pages of my book to scan the yard, searching among the men wearing the FBI's stylish windbreakers. My gaze snagged on the man, taller than the others, with silver hair at his temples and a square jawline.

Holy fuck, he's here.

In all the time since I'd left the FBI, I never thought I'd see Dirk Hopkins again. He'd been the monster of my nightmares, but I figured he'd forgotten me. He won, after all. I'd been chased out of the FBI and he'd gotten away with his crimes. But to see him here, in the courtyard of the Concrete Angels' compound, felt like the biggest betrayal of all. This was my place, my sanctuary as dubious as it might be, and his presence was an insult.

"Are you fuckin' serious?" Dirk waved the warrant at

the AIC. "Who's the sonuvaprick who authorized such a half-ass warrant? You're not gonna find shit if you can't search the residences."

He can't search the residences.

I had to repeat the thought a few times to get my legs to work. If he couldn't search the cabins, I'd be able to hide inside mine until the FBI had gone. I rolled to my feet, or rather staggered like a panicky teenager caught after curfew, and ducked into my cabin.

I heard raised voices and knew the Feds had caught my escape, but I wasn't sticking around to be recognized. I let the door lock behind me as I scrambled into my bedroom, digging out the Glock. I hadn't had the opportunity to defend myself when Hopkins raped me, but I'd be damned before I let him get the jump on me now. I didn't know why he was here. He hadn't been a field agent when I'd worked for him, but I'd shoot him before I let him touch me again.

I settled onto the floor of my bedroom, facing the door. I kept the Glock pointed at the ceiling, but I'd shoot anyone who came through the door. If it was one of the Concrete Angels, I'd apologize later.

****

Scott

When the belligerent guy started yelling about a half-assed warrant, I watched Oriana's face go white as newly fallen snow. I didn't know who he was, but I could guess when she hurtled herself out of her chair and scrambled through the door of her cabin. Apparently I wasn't the only one who noticed her departure because the Feds started yelling and pointed as the door slammed shut behind her.

"Get her back here!"

Belligerent guy waved at the door, but before the Feds

could take more than a couple of steps, I'd stationed myself in front of her door while Abigail repeated the statement about the warrant not covering personal residences. I didn't think Belligerent Guy cared much about the warrant's allowances, but he sure as hell cared about me standing in front of him.

"Get out of the way." His lips peeled back from his teeth in a nasty snarl and I could smell the ham and mustard sandwich he'd eaten earlier that day.

"You know, I'm not real knowledgable about warrants and stuff, but I'm pretty sure it says you can't go in." I tilted my head with a half smile while he seethed. "And I'm sure the woman who lives in this cabin doesn't really want to talk to you."

He tried to gather himself into his official capacity as an agent. "Everyone must be present when we search the premises."

I snorted. "That's bullshit and you know it, Hopkins."

He took a step back and regarded me with narrowed eyes. "How do you know my name?"

I shrugged. "It seemed pretty obvious given Ms. Hunter's reaction to hearing your voice. I figured if she didn't want to be anywhere near someone in the FBI, it'd be you. Given your previous relations and all."

His face crumpled into fury. "Get her ass out here or she'll be arrested."

"For what? Avoiding you?"

"For aiding and abetting criminals in a criminal enterprise." He raised his chin to meet my gaze. We were the same height, but I had a good twenty pounds on him. "If she's here, she's committed a crime by helping you."

"That's not true, Agent Hopkins. Ms. Hunter was hired for her skills as a forensic accountant, and paid fairly for her services. You can check the contract if you like, *ja?*" Loki's voice slithered between us like thin blade.

Hopkins threw his angry gaze at Loki while I set my

laundry basket down on Oriana's chair. I crossed my arms over my chest and braced my feet shoulder-width apart. Sometimes the easiest way to intimidate some belligerent asshole was to stand there, using my size as a roadblock.

"So now she's a whore? That doesn't surprise me. She led me on for months." Hopkins sneered as he waved to the AIC. "Start the search in their barn."

The AIC narrowed his eyes but waved his troops onward. Attila, Calhoun, and the Friar opened the doors where we kept our bikes and waved them in. Calhoun gave them a little bow, a smirk twisting her lips. I idly wondered if they'd seen Roy there near his bike when his buddies came in.

Hopkins turned back to me. "Get out of the way and open that door."

I shrugged and spread my hands. "Can't. Don't have the key."

He narrowed his eyes and looked me up and down as his lip curled. "You're her lastest john, aren't you? What's the matter? Haven't gotten your turn so you won't let anyone in until you blow your wad?"

My anger kindled but I shot him a frown of confusion. "You know, I'd heard women complaining that men only think with their dicks, but I'd never really noticed it until now. But thanks for worrying about my wad."

He must've sensed my anger because he gave me a conspiratorial half-smile. "I've had her, you know. Her pussy was so tight, my dick almost didn't fit. Have you had it yet? It's the sweetest pussy you'll ever fuck."

Fury surged past my carefully held temper and I barely resisted the urge to slam my hand around his throat and squeeze until he stopped breathing. My hand tightened into a fist and I'd settle for a solid punch to his nose. A little blood always changed perspective.

"Who I have sex with is really none of your concern. What are you doing here, Hopkins?"

Oriana's voice hit me the same time her hand curled around my bicep and I checked my forward motion. It was probably a good thing in the long run. I didn't need to get arrested for assault on an officer by this jackass. But he definitely made me want to kick the shit out of him.

"So the bitch comes out of her hidey hole." Hopkins reached for her and she stepped back. "I'm here to arrest the members of the Concrete Angels for possession and trafficking of drugs and arms."

She raised her eyebrows. "Here? On what evidence?"

"Anonymous tip. It's too bad you have to get caught in the middle of it. You used to be a good agent."

Hopkins's tone had gone so patronizing even I wanted to kick him in the balls.

"Yes, I was." She nodded. "I also used to give a shit about what you thought before you raped me, but now your opinion doesn't matter. Your sexual assault killed my respect for you."

I felt more than saw the other agents perk up at her words as they retreated from the barn after having found nothing. *Oh-ho, they didn't know he raped her?* It had been at least two years and she hadn't been a field agent. More than likely the news didn't get around. Or if it did, it was ignored as rumor and hearsay.

Hopkins scowled as he shot a look around at the other men. "I suppose you'll spread your legs for a dirty dog who rides a hog like this guy here, but you said no to me and tried to ruin my career? I always knew you were a slut, but I didn't think you'd go so low as to fuck a biker."

Oriana laughed, a strangled sound boiling with fury. "What is it with men and sex? You think I came to the Concrete Angels to fuck someone?" She snorted and shook her head. "Glory, you're sad. Loki told the truth. He hired me to look into his finances. Sorry you got the wrong intel."

Despite her casual words, I could see her shaking and

her shoulders remained as tight as bow strings. *She's got more courage than half the guys in the club.* Facing her rapist had to be the hardest thing ever and I couldn't imagine what it cost her to do it. Hopkins infuriated me with every low-brow insult, but she let it slide off her like shit off a shingle.

"What's going on, Hopkins?" The AIC closed in on him. "What's she talking about?"

"Nothing. Did you find anything?"

"Negative. The barn and all outbuildings are clear." The AIC looked at me before his gaze shifted to Oriana then back to Hopkins. "Move on to the clubhouse and let's get this over with. You sure the tip that said this place was full of weapons and drugs was good?"

"Hell yeah, it was good. Check the clubhouse." Hopkins strode off toward the front doors in an angry huff and some of my tension left.

"Are you okay?" I brushed Oriana's shoulder with my fingers.

She nodded as she took a shaky breath. "Yeah, well, I'm rather sick to my stomach but I'm okay."

"You were amazing." I gave her a smile. "I'll go make sure he doesn't get into anything he shouldn't."

"Okay." She nodded, her gaze following her rapist as he stormed into the clubhouse. "Is it wrong that I really want to shoot him?"

I laughed. "No, ma'am. I think that's a valid desire. Glory knows I wanted to hit him several times, and not just because of what he did to you." Michael caught my eye and nodded toward the clubhouse. "I gotta go. You gonna be all right?"

"I will when they leave. I'm going to make some tea."

I nodded and kissed her forehead. "I'll be back. Go ahead and set the laundry on the ground. I'll get it when I get back."

She nodded and ducked back inside her cabin. I waited

until the door shut before I trotted for the clubhouse, catching up with Michael.

"She gonna be okay?" He nodded back toward Oriana.

"Yeah, I think so. She's done being social, though. Getting some tea." I held open the clubhouse door for him to precede me through. "I just wanted to make sure the FBI didn't pull some fast shit. When did Abigail get here?"

Michael snorted. "The Shark arrived yesterday evening and spent the whole time holed up in Loki's office prepping for this. I don't know how they knew the FBI would do the raid today, but Loki wanted to be ready."

I shot a look at Loki and Abigail as they stood beside the bar, their attention on the FBI swarming through the room. The people in uniform weren't doing anything too stupid, but I wanted to make sure nothing would happen to Neo's lair. That's where Hopkins and the AIC had gone first.

By the time I got there, Hopkins was snarling something about stupid bikers and half-assed warrants. He brushed past me with a sneer as I looked in the doors of the lair. Neo sat in his chair munching on chips with a video game paused on the monitor behind him. Four other monitors showed security feeds from the barn, the offices in the clubhouse, and the front gate. All the rest of the monitors sat dark. I met Neo's gaze and caught his wink before his expression settled into bored disinterest.

I resisted the urge to laugh as I took in Hopkins's thunderous face. The bastard might have a coronary right here in the compound. Not that I'd mourn him. I doubt Oriana would lose sleep either. Glory knew she'd already lost enough sleep with nightmares from that asshole.

Just the thought of it made the anger surge and I tightened my hands into fists. There had to be a way to take Hopkins down without bringing more heat onto Oriana. And we still hadn't figured out who'd been watching her place, though I'd lay odds on Hopkins.

I scanned the clubhouse, but he was nowhere to be found despite all the bodies wearing FBI jackets.

"Where the fuck is Hopkins?" My feet were already carrying me toward the door before I knew what I was doing. "Michael, he's out there and I bet he's trying to get to her."

My gut sank but my heart blazed with fury as I spotted Hopkins beating on Oriana's door, demanding she come out and face him. I wanted to tackle him to the ground, but so far we hadn't done anything to get us thrown in lockup for the night.

I was still headed for the irate agent when the first bullet ripped through the upper left-hand corner of the door. I skidded to a halt as Hopkins yelped and ducked, scrambling away from the door.

"Shots fired! Shots fired!" The clubhouse emptied like someone had torched the main room, blue windbreakers boiling out into the yard.

"She shot at me!" Hopkins yelled as he got to his feet a few strides from the door. "Arrest her!"

The agents who hadn't seen the shot looked at each other and Schnoz and I played along. We shared a surprised look before returning our gazes to him.

"What are you talking about?" I frowned and shook my head. "Who shot at you?"

"That bitch, Hunter!" He pointed at the door just as it opened and Oriana stepped out. "Arrest her."

"What's going on?" She held a steaming mug in her hands.

"You're under arrest, you slut!" Hopkins reversed his direction and came for Oriana. I tried to intercept, but it turned out I didn't have to.

In a move straight out of a spy movie, Oriana set down her mug on the window planter, swung her arm behind her, and came up with a subcompact Glock 43, cupping the butt of the gun with her left hand. She held it in front of her steadily, her focus on Hopkins, who skidded to a halt no more than ten feet from her.

"Stop." Her voice could've frozen boiling water. Hell, my testicles tried to climb back up into my body cavity at the coldness in it. "That's close enough. One more step and I'll blow a hole through you."

"You just threatened an FBI agent." Hopkins sneered.

"No, I just threatened the man who was beating on the door of my residence, harassing me after raping me two years ago. So, back the fuck off, Dirk. You remember my gun range scores, don't you?" Her eyes narrowed. "You used to tease me about a number-cruncher not needing to keep up her markswomanship. I recall you being amazed at how many times I hit center mass. Wanna test me now? I got a damn good target and you're not as far away as the paper ones at the range."

"What's she talking about, Hopkins?" The AIC had his hands out to placate someone, but I didn't think he knew which person to placate.

"Nothing, she's crazy. Arrest her."

"He's a rapist and if he gets closer to me, it'll be self-defense. And I don't shoot to wound." She never looked away from Hopkins and the muzzle of the Glock never wavered. "He raped me. I was an FBI agent, one of you in Denver, and he raped me in a broom closet. I was one of you and none of you stood up for me. He was too upstanding. Look how upstanding he is now."

"Arrest her, for god's sake. What are you waiting for?"

I moved to flank Oriana, careful not to get in her line of sight. Michael and Dollhouse stood beside me as the Friar, Attila, Karma, and Calhoun filled in on Oriana's other side. From what I could see, their expressions held no humor, just determination and disdain.

"You can't arrest her. She hasn't done anything wrong." Abigail came up behind Loki and tilted her head.

"She threatened an officer of the law."

"No, technically you broke the law, Agent Hopkins." Loki waved at the door behind Oriana. "Your warrant said you could search our public buildings, but not the residences. And you where trying to break into one of our homes. As I understand it, Ms. Hunter has the right to defend her residence from unlawful entrance. Plus, I do believe she filed a police report after she was raped and they ran the rape kit. That means all they'd need to convict you is a DNA sample, right? A cheek swab would probably do the trick, but blood would work, too."

I didn't know there'd been a rape kit run, but Loki had his ways and I didn't really want to know how he got the information.

"Is this true, Hopkins?" The AIC had shifted his attention to the jackass practically frothing at the mouth. I was tempted to get a rabies shot just looking at him. "Did you rape this woman?"

"Of course not. She's trying to ruin my career." Hopkins scoffed and gestured to Oriana. "It's just the ranting of a biker's slut."

Man, I was getting really tired of him insulting her. Part of me hoped she squeezed the trigger and shot his balls off.

"As far as I can tell, Dirk, I didn't ruin your career in the Old Boys' club. You seem like you're doin' fine." She kept her focus on him and I kinda hoped he'd push her far enough to shoot him.

"A simple DNA test will prove it, Agent Cisneros."

Loki sounded so damn reasonable, but I didn't trust him when he wore his amused half-smile. That sent up all sorts of warning flags for me.

Apparently, Cisneros wasn't stupid either because he shook his head and waved at Hopkins. "Let's go, Hopkins. We've served the warrant and searched the place. It's time to go. Leave the woman alone."

Hopkins snarled and pointed at Oriana. "This isn't

over."

"Let it go, Hopkins. Get him out of here." Cisneros waved at one of the other agents to collect Hopkins. "Everybody out."

"Thanks for dropping by, agents." Loki waved with a genial smile. "Come back again when you can't stay as long, *ja*?"

Hopkins scowled and yanked his arm out of reach of the escorting agents, but he stomped out of the compound. Cisneros nodded to Loki and waved at the rest to leave. Oriana didn't lower her weapon until Hopkins had cleared the gate.

"Fuck." Her whispered epithet carried to my ears as her shoulders bowed and her head dropped.

"Hey, I got you." I touched her shoulder. "Do you want some more tea?"

"Yes, thanks."

I nodded and headed for the clubhouse. Michael filled in to my space as the FBI started to clear out, and I knew she'd be safe while I stepped away. She'd been so strong it made my heart swell. Hopkins thought he could threaten her and the Concrete Angels stepped in as backup. I couldn't have been more proud of my crew.

CHAPTER SIXTEEN

Oriana

The gates closed behind the FBI and I tried to get my body to relax.

He's gone.

Relief made my knees turn to mush and I damn near crumpled onto the lawn chair I'd set under the Ponderosa pine outside my cabin. *He's gone, and I'm home.* It seemed like an odd thing to say given the short time I'd been with the Concrete Angels, but each and every member had stood up with me and faced down Agent Hopkins and his frustrated fury. I had a family, now, though a very unconventional one.

I'd wanted retribution on Hopkins for two years now, ever since he raped me and I'd left the FBI where no one had my back. This wasn't what I'd had in mind, but might have actually been a better result. Rape was about power, and Hopkins had been impotent here in the compound. The search warrant had yielded nothing—no guns, no drugs— and none of us were doing anything illegal. Hell, the Friar had been tinkering with his bike and Scott had been doing laundry. *Might be weird for a guy to do laundry, but still legal in the state of Colorado.*

Agent Hopkins had been powerless and it felt fuckin' awesome to watch him twitch over it.

Buh-bye, Faleena.

I scrubbed my face and let out my breath in a long sigh.

"How are you holding up, Oriana?"

I glanced up to find Michael standing in front of me, his expression filled with concern as he looked me over. I'd holstered the Glock behind my back again, but my hand still shook.

"Exhausted, but good, I think." I tried to give him a smile.

"You stood your ground well, I thought." His smile was far better than mine.

"It helped that the rest of you stood with me."

He shrugged. "Yeah, well, we don't leave anyone hanging out to dry. That asshole was threatening you and that wasn't cool."

I nodded. "Y'all are the first people to stand up for me. It was a welcome surprise."

Michael scowled. "That's wrong on so many levels. Sometimes I wonder what the fuck is wrong with humans."

It was a strange thing to say, but I couldn't argue with him. Humans could be the most messed up thing on the planet. I wrapped my arms around myself and sighed, hoping the shivering would stop soon. I knew it was in reaction to the adrenaline surge, but it made me feel like a junkie coming off a binge.

"I don't think you'll see Agent Hopkins again."

That was another odd thing to say and I shot him a skeptical look. "How do you figure?"

He shrugged. "Just a feeling I have."

Scott returned with a new steaming cup of tea and Michael rose, clapping him on the shoulder. He didn't say anything, but they shared a significant look I couldn't read before Scott sat down on the lawn chair next to me.

"How are you feeling?" He handed me the mug of tea.

I bit my lip. "I think I'm okay. Really frickin' tired, but good."

"Yeah." He nodded, a smile curling his lips. "Yeah, you look good. Better than good. Sexy."

I laughed and patted his thigh with one hand. "Oh good. I was worried I hadn't gotten my sexy on for the FBI."

"Oh, you did, but they were too worried about finding shit that wasn't here. They couldn't see the sexy." He bumped my shoulder with his hard bicep. "But I could. You know we have your back now, right? You're one of the Concrete Angels and we look after our own."

I nodded. "Yeah, I know, honorary member."

"No, full member, with benefits and backup and protection." His expression had shifted to earnestness. "The shit you did, the strength you showed. That made you a full member. It's what we're lookin' for in the Scooters. They're trying to get the strength and conviction you have. You're there, darlin'."

"You really still want me to stay? Even with my panic attacks and my nightmares, and my past?" I searched his gaze, needing that one last bit of reassurance.

He cupped my cheek with one big hand. "I want you to stay, Oriana. One night, a week, or hell, stay forever. Wear my patch, be my woman, let me be your man, forever. We're good together. Whadaya say?"

I thought about the times I'd spent with him and this crew of unruly and unusual bikers. Were they white hats? Definitely not, but they weren't completely black hats, either, and I'd long ago thrown off my halo. But these men and woman who made up the Concrete Angels had more heart than most ordinary people, and they stood behind each other like family, a family who cared. I'd done much worse with ordinary folks.

"You'll wear my patch?" I raised an eyebrow. "For real, no foolin'?"

"Hell yeah. No foolin'."

I tilted my head and squinted my eyes. "You know, I think I'd like to see that on you. And I'd like my own jacket to wear." I sipped my tea as I waited for his reaction.

He paused, his eyebrows going up. "You want a jacket?"

"Well, yeah. If I'm a full member of the Concrete Angels, I deserve a jacket to wear when we ride around on your bike."

"You said you don't know how to ride a bike."

"You said you'd teach me."

A slow grin curled his lips. "Hell yeah, I'll teach you. Anytime you want."

I nodded. "I still want my own car, which we left at my apartment when we got my stuff."

He shot me a smug smile. "No, we didn't."

"What?"

"Schnoz took Dollhouse down to your apartment the next morning and drove it back up here. It's parked behind the barn." He dug around in his front pocket and pulled out my car keys. "I think Dollhouse even filled the tank and the Friar changed the oil. You should have that checked more regularly. It was a quart low."

I snorted. Car maintenance hadn't been high on my list of priorities after the rape, although given my need for independence, it should've been higher.

"Thanks."

"Yeah, anytime." He handed me the keys and wrapped his warm hand around mine. "How about we get something to eat? I think Grub is making Chicken Parmesan tonight."

I pocketed the keys and grabbed my teacup. "Yeah, I'm kinda starving. But that's not all I'm hungry for." I licked my lips and winked at him.

The surprise on his face was downright comical, but the cocky smirk soon took over. "Hell yeah. I'm totally up for dessert after."

****

Oriana

I'd just finished up the last of my modifications on Loki's financial records a little over a week later when someone knocked on my office door. Since I'd become a full-fledged member of the Concrete Angels, Loki decided I needed to have an office in the clubhouse where I could be close to the leadership when it came to money matters. *And they needed the guest cabin back.* Since their financial records and accounts were a ridiculous jumbled mess, I'd have at least several months' worth of work just to get untangled and organized. *Gotta love job security.*

"Yeah, come in." I swiveled around in my chair to see Michael leaning in the door. "What's up, Michael? Come in."

"Are you at a breaking point?"

I snorted. "If I wasn't getting paid to look at this mess you call your financial accounts, I might be. Why?"

He raised his eyebrows before he cracked a grin. "Oh, no, that's not what I meant, but that's good to hear. No, I meant can you come out to the lair? There's something you need to see."

"Okay." My gut sank. What had Michael so serious? This couldn't be good. I rose and followed him out to Neo's lair. They'd thoughtfully left the door wide open for me. I'd gotten better at being in dark spaces, but I still didn't like his blackout room.

Loki, Neo, Michael, Dollhouse and the woman named Viper were all there, looking at some of the screens, but they all turned around when I stepped in the door. I wondered where Scott was, but the greetings I got from the others made me feel welcome.

"Hey, Numbers, thanks for joining us." Neo had become a good friend, aware of my foibles and impressed with my computer wizardry, at least with respect to financial records.

"Hey. What's going on? Michael said there was something I needed to see?" I couldn't call him Schnoz no matter how long I'd known him. He'd always be Michael to me.

"Yeah, so Viper and I have been working on where those cameras and mikes in your apartment were transmitting to, and there's good news and bad news."

My shoulders tightened up and my gut sank. *Oh this should be awesome.* Nothing like having my daily routine broadcast to a fraternity of assholes in the FBI or any other agency in the federal government. *Although I bet the NSA already knows all about me.*

"Let's start with the bad news."

Neo nodded. "Actually, the news is both good and bad. These feeds were being sent directly to Dirk Hopkins's home computer. I traced his IP address. He was keeping an eye on you for some reason, not the whole FBI. In fact, I'm pretty sure the FBI didn't know he was monitoring you at all."

Neo was right, that was both good and bad news. Then he threw me for a loop.

"How long have you been friends with Melrose?"

I blinked and thought back. "Uh, I don't know. About fifteen months, I guess. Why?"

"Because that's when the feeds started." Viper exchanged a look with Dollhouse. "We think she brought the cameras and mikes in. Or she let someone in who could set them up."

My stomach cramped and bile worked its way up my throat. *Holy shit, that bitch has been playing me for more than a year!* I pressed a hand to my belly and swallowed hard. How could she do that to me? She'd been my first friend after the assault, but it turned out she wasn't a friend at all. She'd set me up from the beginning.

"That weaselly, scum-sucking bitch." My voice was rough enough to grind up gravel. "Was she undercover FBI too?"

Neo shook his head. "We don't think so. We can't find her in any of their records. Maybe she really just was Roy's girlfriend, but I'll keep looking. Something about her seems hinky."

Hinky was an understatement. And the Concrete Angels wondered why I had trust issues.

"But watching you wasn't the only thing agent Dirk Hopkins was up to." Viper clicked a few keys on another keyboard and a new set of images came up on another screen. "Apparently, Dirk could take the nickname John Hopkins because he frequents several seedy brothels in Denver and Littleton. He seems to like it rough enough that he's been kicked out of a few for beating the shit out of and damn near raping the prostitutes there. Someone ought to cut his dick off."

"You won't get any argument from me." I scowled at the images of the bruised and broken sex workers when I noticed a creepy detail. "Hey wait. Am I imagining things, or do all these women kinda look like me?"

No one said anything and I turned my head to look at them. Michael and Loki held grim expressions while Neo's face was carefully blank, and Viper's had settled into fury. Dollhouse met my gaze and nodded, her eyes sad.

"Yeah, we noticed that. We think he's become a serial rapist and he's fixated on you."

"Holy fuck." My stomach sank to somewhere around my ankles. "Please say someone has caught him and they know about this."

"Not yet, but they will." Neo's voice held tight anger.

"I'm gonna release all this evidence to the news outlet anonymously. Someone's gonna get the scoop of a lifetime and Hopkins is going down."

"What about Roy? He was undercover FBI and Hopkins's friend." I shook off the unease of Dirk's unhealthy obsession with me.

"Oh, Roy is missing." Loki wore a sad expression until I met his gaze. Only smug satisfaction looked back at me. "He slipped out during the raid, but we caught up with him when he went camping."

"What did y'all do to him?" I wasn't really sure I wanted to know.

Loki shrugged. "I don't exactly know. He was still alive when we left him." But from how he said it, I didn't think Roy remained among the living. "You know there have been a lot of forest fires all over Colorado this year. Dangerous to go out camping now."

Oh, shit.

Loki shrugged with a half-smile. "I'm sure he'll be fine. He's a big boy, after all, and an FBI agent. He can take care of himself."

Yeah, I'd believe that when I managed to meet an Archangel face-to-face. Michael shifted and met my gaze with an odd look. It seemed to be a mixture of amusement and surprise. *What's that about?*

"Hey laddies, something is happening. If yer done ogling the data, maybe you should come out here." Attila waved at us to come out into the main room of the clubhouse.

"What's going on?" Dollhouse slipped past me before I could turn. "Are we getting visited by the FBI again?"

"Kinda."

That was Scott's voice. I hadn't seen him since this morning after we showered. He'd said he had a couple of errands to run down in Denver, and while that wasn't unusual, I really missed him. I stepped out of Neo's lair and stopped.

The entire host of the Concrete Angels gathered in the main room of the clubhouse with Scott standing at the center. He had a wide grin on his face and held two large pieces of leather clothing. *Oh, glory, this isn't going to be a BDSM sort of thing, is it?*

"Hey, Numbers. You wanna come over here? I got somethin' for you."

Did I want to know what it was? I'd never seen Scott look so predatory or sexy before, and that's saying a lot considering he was a cocky biker through and through. I shot a look around my new family, trying to gauge what was happening from their expressions. Some wore anticipation. Others settled into mild interest. Dollhouse looked excited while Karma wore satisfaction. Loki kept his enigmatic half-smile, but Michael appeared hopeful.

So there's anticipation of hopeful satisfaction with a dash of excitement. Great.

I smoothed my hands down on my jean-clad thighs and went to meet Scott. I stopped in front of him and his eyes filled up with love. It warmed my chest but I resisted the urge to move my hands. *Be cool, Hunter.*

"I'm not too good with words and half the time I say the wrong shit, but Schnoz says that's part of my charm." He shot me a self-deprecating smile as the audience laughed. "So rather than get all wordy, I'm just gonna do this."

I'd held it together so far but I totally lost my composure when he dropped to one knee.

"Ms. Oriana Hunter, aka Numbers, will you be my old lady and wear my patch?"

The room collectively held its breath as he held up one piece of the leather clothing. I realized it was a leather jacket, smaller than most, with the gargoyle on the flaming bike emblem of the Concrete Angels on the back. At the top it read "NUMBERS" and the rocker below read

"Property of Scott Free."

I reached out to take the jacket, admiring its style and color. Black, silky-smooth leather with zippered pockets and cut in a feminine style. I met his gaze as I swung it around my shoulders and shoved my arms through the sleeves. It fit perfectly.

I debated making him wait for my answer, teasing my big, bad, cocky biker. But in the end, I decided he didn't deserve the fear of my rejection.

"Yeah, Scott. I'll be your lady, old or otherwise, and I'll wear your patch."

My heart blazed as bright as his smile and excitement made it pound as he held up the other piece of leather. "Help me put this on?"

He handed me his cut. I recognized it, but the emblems had changed. The top still read "SCOTT FREE" but the rocker now read "Property of Numbers." It was a silly change, but it made me feel like I finally belonged, even more so than the rocker on my own jacket. I held it up and he slipped his hands through the arm holes, settling it on his broad shoulders.

"Damn, you look sexy."

I had no idea where the words came from, but the whole room exploded in cheers and whoops of joy. Even Loki wore an unusually contented smile. *Say what you like about Loki, but I think he's a born romantic.* Scott turned around and wrapped me in his warm arms. I leaned into him with a happy sigh.

"I love you, Scott."

He pushed me back and met my gaze, searching my eyes for something. "Yeah? Well that's damn good news because I love you, too, Oriana. Whadaya say you stay with me forever?"

"You sure that's what you want?"

"Hell yeah. I want to be the one you trust to have your back and defend you against assailants when you're most vulnerable."

He remembered what I'd needed the night after I had my first panic attack. Tears of joy started in my eyes and I gave him a tremulous smile as I wiped my face.

"You've got yourself a deal."

He whooped and threw himself into my arms, which was a pretty good feat considering he was bigger than me. But as I wrapped around his broad back, his head on my chest, I thanked my lucky stars I'd had the opportunity for my forever cocky biker encounter.

EPILOGUE

Karma

"Are there more troubles on the way for the local FBI office? Special Agent Dirk Hopkins has been indicted on multiple counts of embezzlement of federal funds for private use, illegal and unauthorized wire taps on a former employee, and multiple sexual harassment charges from female coworkers. Hopkins allegedly used the federal funds to pay prostitutes to look like his former employee, a woman who accused him of rape two years ago. While the employee chose to leave the FBI when her accusations were swept under the rug, Hopkins remained in a position of authority over several other women employees and allegedly made unwanted advances toward them. The FBI has yet to comment about the allegations against Hopkins, but they did have this to say."

"All accusations are being fully investigated at this time."

"It's about time!" Dollhouse yelled at the TV as she looked up from our pool game. "Those jackasses should've hung him by his balls when Numbers first said something."

I was inclined to agree. Numbers definitely had to put up with a lot of shit because of Special Agent Dirk Hopkins and his asshole buddy, Arnold Eisenburg AKA Roy.

"Your shot, Karma."

I nodded and lined up the cue ball with the purple seven.

"Wildfires raged across the state again today, swelling to fifty-five thousand acres. While firefighters from four states battle the blazes, it turned out to be more deadly than usual. Fire crew spotted a body when clearing debris."

"Yeah, we'd already marked the line and were clearing some of the charred trees when we found it. Looks like a camper got caught by surprise when the wind shifted last night." The firefighter speaking was kinda cute. "These fires can move fast when the winds shift. This poor guy probably never had a chance."

The camera focused on the anchorperson again. "This marks the second body found after a drastic shift in wind conditions along the Western Slope. So far the police haven't released the name of the victim, but it's thought to be a member of a local motorcycle club who recently went missing while camping."

I tuned out the rest of the report as I made my shot. Both Special Agent Dirk Hopkins and Roy got handed their Karma and I didn't have to do a damn thing. I definitely agreed with Dollhouse.

"Fuck yeah, it's about time."

THE END

AUTHOR'S NOTE

A lot of people have asked me why I entitled this story My Forever Cocky Biker Encounter. Back when I started writing this story in May 2018, Romancelandia was going through a rough patch. A would-be actress and author tried to trademark the word "Cocky" and went after other, previously published authors, threatening them with legal action if they didn't take the word "Cocky" out of their titles. A lawyer came out of retirement, there were court hearings, and in the end, the cocky would-be author withdrew her trademark petition.

Of course authors and game makers jumped on the bandwagon and tried to trademark "Forever", "Biker", "Rebellion", and "Encounter," respectively. All of them were fought and shot down. But that's why the title of this tale is My Forever Cocky Biker Encounter. Happy reading.

Siobhan

DUDE WITH A COOL CAR
CONCRETE ANGELS MC, BOOK 2
SNEEK PEEK

Cooper DeVille, US Marshal

Being undercover has its perks. I get to do stuff the day-to-day me would never experience. Like infiltrating the Concrete Angels Motorcycle Club and meeting Karma, the gorgeous Enforcer of the MC. Being handcuffed to her bed is a dream, but that's the problem with undercover work. Everything I'm doing here is only half true. The Concrete Angels—and Karma—are connected to Backlog, a shadow organization infiltrating law enforcement. The Fed undercover here before me was Backlog's bitch, and now he's dead. I have to determine which side of this fight the Concrete Angels are on... before Karma comes to bite me in ways I won't enjoy.

Karma, Concrete Angels' Enforcer

You bet your ass, I'm that karma, the one people pray never catches up to them. But my own karma has found me, seeing as the hunky P.I. who drove into the MC compound with his cool car is my Goddess-chosen true mate. But as my luck—and the Goddess' sense of humor—would have it, Cooper's an undercover US Marshal trying to ferret out our connection to a group called Backlog. Would've been nice to know before I took him to bed and discovered he's the best damn submissive this Madam could want, because I don't deal well with liars. And no one's happy when Karma's pissed. But Backlog has Cooper in its sights, and to survive... my mate might just have to die.

OTHER BOOKS BY SIOBHAN MUIR

Queen Bitch of the Callowwood Pack
Her Devoted Vampire
Second Chance Succubus
Wildfire's Heart
Darwin's Evolution

Bad Boys of Beta Squad Series
Bronco's Rough Ride
The Navy's Ghost
Rimshot's Hard Target
Bam-Bam's Inked Hart
Deli's Take Out

Cloudburst Colorado Series
A Hell Hound's Fire
The Beltane Witch
Christmas I.C.E. Magic
Cloudburst Ice Magic
Cloudburst Coffee & Spa

Concrete Angels MC Series
My Forever Cocky Biker Encounter

Rifts Series
Take the Reins
A Centaur's Solstice Wish
In Death's Shadow

The Ivory Road Serial
A Walk in the Sand
Outback Dreams

Triple Star Ranch Series
Rope a Falling Star
Star Light, Star Bright

Warbler Peninsula Series
Order of the Dragon
The Valkyrie's Sword
Burning Yuletide

Coming Soon
Dude With a Cool Car (Concrete Angels MC #2)
Angel Ink (Concrete Angels MC #3)
Courting the Dragon Widow (Cloudburst Colorado #6)
Star Spangled Banner (Triple Star Ranch #3)

ABOUT THE AUTHOR

Siobhan Muir lives in Cheyenne, Wyoming, with her husband, two daughters, and a vegetarian cat she swears is a shape-shifter, though he's never shifted when she can see him. When not writing, she can be found looking down a microscope at fossil fox teeth, pursuing her other love, paleontology. An avid reader of science fiction/fantasy, her husband gave her a paranormal romance for Christmas one year, and she was hooked for good.

In previous lives, Siobhan has been an actor at the Colorado Renaissance Festival, a field geologist in the Aleutian Islands, and restored inter-planetary imagery at the USGS. She's hiked to the top of Mount St. Helens and to the bottom of Meteor Crater.

Siobhan writes kick-ass adventure with hot sex for men and women to enjoy. She believes in happily ever after, redemption, and communication, all of which you will find in her paranormal romance stories.

Connect with Siobhan online at:
https://www.siobhanmuir.com
https://www.siobhanmuir.com/siobhans-blog
https://twitter.com/SiobhanMuir
http://pinterest.com/siobhanmuir.35
https://www.facebook.com/siobhan.muir.35

32474896R00122

Made in the USA
Lexington, KY
03 March 2019